# HOSTAGE

## AN EVERYDAY HEROES WORLD NOVEL

## JAS T. WARD

Published by KB Worlds LLC.

Cover Design by Designs by Carolann

Editing by Rogena Mitchell-Jones & Colleen Snibson

Two Red Pens Editing www.tworedpens.com

Formatting by Rogena Mitchell-Jones, RMJ Manuscript Service

Published in the United States of America

# INTRODUCTION

Dear Reader,

Welcome to the Everyday Heroes World!

I'm so excited you've picked up this book! *Hostage* is a book based on the world I created in my *USA Today* bestselling Everyday Heroes Series. While I may be finished writing this series (*for now*), various authors have signed on to keep them going. They will be bringing you all-new stories in the world you know while allowing you to revisit the characters you love.

This book is entirely the work of the author who wrote it. While I allowed them to use the world I created and may have assisted in some of the plotting, I took no part in the writing or editing of the story. All praise can be directed their way.

I truly hope you enjoy *Hostage*. If you're interested in finding more authors who have written in the KB Worlds, you can visit www.kbworlds.com.

Thank you for supporting the writers in this project and me.
Happy Reading,
K. Bromberg

"*M*s. Lily?"

Lily Devenmore looked up as one of the Academy's first graders placed a plastic-wrapped, homemade cookie on her desk. She took the treat, examined it, and smiled at the girl. "Thank you. Did your mom make this, Tiffany?"

The student gave her a wide, gap-toothed smile. "She did! She put it in my lunch."

Lily stepped back and raised a brow in amusement. "Is it because you don't want me to tell her about getting in trouble today?"

The sweet smile fell. "Maybe."

Lily chuckled as she walked the little girl to the door. "And did you think this would get you out of trouble?"

"Um. Maybe?"

Glancing to the road, Lily saw Tiffany's mother waiting next to a Mercedes SUV parked in the circle drive in front of the mansion renovated into a private school. Sighing, she gave the girl a wink. "Go. You did wrong in stabbing Jimmy in the arm with a pencil. But the cookie is nice. You still have to apologize to him."

"He deserved it, Ms. Lily." She pointed to her mouth. "He said the tooth fairy wasn't real." She rocked on her heels. "Boys are stupid."

Lily leaned forward. "But I'll keep it from your mom this time as long as you don't do it again. Deal?"

The big smile returned when she learned of the reprieve. "Yes, ma'am. Thank you!" Tiffany ran, and Lily watched as she reached her mom. The woman waved to Lily, and she returned one. Lily watched the two wistfully. Then she returned to her chair, ripped open the cookie, propped her heels up on the desk, crossing her ankles, and took a big bite.

Lily had never developed a love for baking. Oh sure, she and her sisters were all taught the skill by their mother. Her older sister, Emma, made desserts that rivaled any professional pastry chef. But Lily? She'd rather curl up with a book than a mixing bowl. Books helped her get past the pain of losing not only her parents but their older brother as a young girl. An all too common tragic occurrence at "work." Both she and her sisters carried on the family tradition of working on the Grid. A secret army organized centuries ago to fight the factors of Hell—demons and things of the best blockbuster creature features.

She fondly recalled the challenge for Bounce, the leader of that army, in raising three teenage girls after they spend the first few years with a foster family. They were surrounded by tall, fanged immortal guys who made any book boyfriend look and seem boring. The three Devenmore girls had a new crush on one of the heroes more often than other girls their age changed hair bows and put on a fresh coat of nail polish. Her sister Emma had married and now had children with one such badass. Rose, their youngest sister, married a member of the army who served on the Grid in cooperation with the military. And Lily? She'd never had a serious relationship. She came close once with a Breaker, the immortal fighters on the Grid, but it was doomed from the moment it started. Too much baggage and history. They then became friends. She'd take that over getting her heart broken by being rejected and unwanted any day.

Other than baking, another ability her sisters excelled at was marriage. Children. The whole white-picket-fence shebang. It wasn't that Lily didn't want a family of her own. She dreamed of a houseful of children running around—only one thing missing in making it come true.

A man.

One who would accept Lily as she was. Loud. Bold and in his face at the drop of a hat. Lily learned at a very early age that her personality was a quality she could control. Her looks? Her body and its shape—not. She spent the majority of her teenage years fighting the image of herself in the mirror. She longed to fit in Emma's hand-me-downs only to send them down the sibling train for Rose to wear eventually. Both her sisters got whistles and offers of dates from the boys. Lily only received the opposite. Cruel insults. Boys cupped their hands around their mouths to make moo noises. Did it hurt? Yes. Did she show that pain? No.

Over the years, she had learned to shove her emotions down, and for a few years, she suffered bulimia. Only her older sister, Emma, knew. When Emma discovered it, she was the only one to help Lily conquer it. Let her sisters be the supermodels. Lily didn't resent them a single bit. Genetics were nothing more than DNA strands. And something she had no power to change.

Finishing the cookie, she picked up her phone to enter its calories in her fitness app. She learned to love herself despite herself years ago, an out-there personality she no longer hid but wore as armor. She worked her way up from a librarian at the San Francisco library to helping her friend William Bailey run the Academy. Lily loved her job. The kids. Even the administration side of it. She became a damn good principal. Her double degrees in English studies and education were hard-earned and now fully utilized. Her attitude wasn't her only strength. Her sharp mind assisted in the job of handling life.

Who needed a man—marriage or romance. She had all she needed. The long hours and demands left little time for a relationship. Good riddance to the hassle it brought into her life.

As she placed her phone on the desk, it lit up with an incoming text message.

Speaking of hassle.

Swearing under her breath, she picked the device up and stuck her tongue out at the name of the sender.

"Your reports are due, Ms. Devenmore. Today." Ah, Evan O'Brien. Good looking. Strong. Tall. Handsome as a movie star. And a real pain in the ass. Lily smirked as her thumbs hovered over the phone to text back. But rather than reply, she closed the app and stood. Her reports were ready to be filed—a matter of scanning them and sending them on their way by the structured deadline via email.

"Where would be the fun in that?" she asked herself as she scooped up her keys and the backpack she used as a purse.

Email would deprive Lily of the chance to needle Evan, the activity usually the highlight of Lily's week.

---

EVAN O'BRIEN HEARD her voice from across the communication room of the Grid. It was boldly loud. The sound of it thudded against his blooming headache like a tom-tom. Tonight began the first shift of the week at work, which meant reports from the prior week were due. Even in a secret army fighting the forces of Hell, an organized structure for operation demanded efficient maintenance to run smoothly. As second in command, Evan took the role seriously. He reinforced the rules and coordinated rosters of duty. He wrangled the fighters—both human and supernatural—with an ironclad figurative fist of command. He was very good at it and enjoyed the task. It left little time for anything else in his life. He was fine with that—relationships and friends placed a complication on his existence. Evan had neither the patience nor spare capacity to deal with more beyond the demands of work.

Standing to avoid the woman marching toward him, he failed

to escape when she stepped in his path and slapped sheets of papers against his chest. "Here are your reports, ass stick."

Lily Devenmore. A full-figured woman with dark wavy hair and deep green eyes. She looked at Evan with disdain and irritation each time they crossed paths—which, considering she and a retired immortal by the name of William Bailey ran the Grid-affiliated Edge Academy for Gifted Children, occurred more than either of them liked.

"You could have emailed these, Ms. Devenmore. I believe I stated so in my text." He took the paper and attempted to sidestep around her. No luck. She moved to aggravate him by obstructing his path. He let out a slow exhale to brace himself for the latest confrontation before he took a sip of coffee. It's not like he could step outside for air to get away as a ruse. Not until after sundown, anyway. He and many others on the Grid were "allergic" to the sun—a.k.a. bursting into flames in UV light. "Is there anything else you need for the Academy?"

Lily crossed her arms with a smile. "Other than making your life hell? And that's not for the benefit of the school. That's for me and my enjoyment. So, not really. I don't need anything for school."

Evan kept his eyes on her face—ignoring how the movement of her arms lifted her ample breasts to accentuate her luscious figure.

Evan lowered his mug and met her gaze. "Consider your goal for the day accomplished. Have a pleasant one, Ms. Devenmore." Again, he attempted an escape. And once more, she thwarted it.

"Lily. I have a first name. It's Lily. And I told you over and over, call me Lily. Everyone else does." She moved in close, and now those breasts were brushing his chest. She smiled sweetly. "Say it with me, Evan. Should I spell it for you? I'm helpful like that. L.I.L.Y. It's a very simple name. Try it."

*Do not let this woman push buttons. Give an inch, and she'll take a yard.* Evan hooded his gaze. "I am well aware of your name, as I am of all the personnel in my charge. Now, excuse me. I have a meeting with Bounce." The worst excuse to use. Since Lily was his boss's charge since her teenage years, she'd have few qualms about following him to the man's office. Evan knew for a fact Bounce wasn't at work. He was at his nightclub, Club Bounce, for the evening.

Able to step around her on the next attempt, he gave her no additional attention even as she stood behind him to watch him go. After a sip of coffee, the delicate scent of her skin that was left behind left his senses.

Reaching his office, Evan dropped heavily into the chair behind his desk. Eyes tracked personnel moving about their duties for the day in the hallway as he brought a hand up to scrub over his face. Lily Devenmore got under his skin like no other. He also knew she was aware of it and enjoyed digging deep into him as entertainment.

"E?"

His hand dropped and found Taylor, one of the healers, standing in his doorway. Taylor was a pretty brunette with bright blue eyes and the calm, kind nature required by her position in Grid's medical clinic. "Hey, Taylor, what can I do for you?"

She entered the office and closed the door behind her. "Some of us are headed to Club Bounce for the night. It's eighties night, and even though it's lame, it's fun. I thought perhaps you'd want to go?" She pointed behind her. "I noticed you through the doorway. You appeared tense, and I don't know"—she lifted a shoulder and lowered her gaze with a soft smile—"you never get out or away from work." She bubbled out a laugh. "And I would be remiss in my job if I didn't look out for one of our own." Her eyes drifted back up to his. "And I thought you could go with me to the club." She smiled sweetly. "Together."

Evan listened as Taylor indirectly and indiscreetly asked him out for a date. He knew where the conversation led. It would not be the first time nor the last. It happened often. When one worked in close quarters with coworkers, relationships were bound to develop. Many dated others and some even found love to move on to marriage.

Evan, however, was not that type. In fact, in all of his immortal time being a part of the Grid, he never partook in the romantic practice. Sure, he had a random hookup but never with anyone at work. It complicated things. His job contained enough stress without adding another person—one he would neglect with zero doubt—into the equation.

He knew Taylor meant well, and he didn't wish to hurt her feelings. It would make working together awkward. "Thank you, Taylor. I've too much work to do. Maybe another time." A lie. There would be no other time he'd take her up on it. Or anyone.

Those blue eyes nailed him with scrutiny for a moment before she pressed her lips together with a nod. "Okay. Have a good night."

She went to leave, and he called out as she exited, "Can you close the door, please?"

That got him another nod, and the door closed.

2

"*L*ily? Is that you?"

Lily stood in line at the small organic grocery store a mile from her house. She'd been absentmindedly watching the sunset fall over San Francisco Bay and the Golden Gate Bridge beyond the window. Someone calling out to her broke into her thoughts.

Angling to see who, she smiled to see Desi Whitman one cash register over. "Hey!" Lily paid for her items as Desi did the same, and they met in the middle near the store's exit. Each gave the other a one-arm hug, their bags of groceries on the opposite arm bumping together. "What are you doing in San Fran? Don't tell me that Sunnyville doesn't have organic grocery stores. I would think that cute tiny town would have everything."

Desi rolled her eyes. "Reznor had a police convention here in the city. He insisted I come along to get away from the business. He didn't even make us a reservation at a hotel that allowed *dogs*! I went off on him, but then he made it clear he wanted me to rest, to give *him* all my attention. That man is worse than a pet, but he also knows I can't resist those puppy dog eyes that he pulls off so well."

Lily and Desi had met a year or so ago through a California

pet rescue organization. Desi had donated grooming services for the animals up for adoption, and Lily made ad copy for the posts placed on social media and the organization's website. Together with a photographer who offered services, adoptions skyrocketed with the adorable stories and human-like bios of the animals. In the process, she and Desi formed a friendship. Desi occasionally sent Lily invites to dinner or a visit to Sunnyville. Lily declined each one. If there was one thing she avoided more than anything else, being a third person with a couple on a date would be it. It was bad enough when she spent time with one of her sisters in their homes.

Desi's boyfriend was a former San Fran SWAT officer who left the city's force to work with the police department in Sunnyville. And though Lily made excuses not to visit Desi and meet the man, she drooled more than once over the pictures of him on Desi's social media. "Maybe I can take you and him out to dinner one night this week. Or lunch, whichever works for you two."

Desi gave Lily a friendly smile. "Yes, let's do that. But tell me"—her face took on the edge of apparent wicked curiosity as she let a couple pass by—"will it be a threesome or a foursome?" She wiggled a brow, and Lily couldn't help but laugh.

"If you mean, will I have a date? No. There's no one." What Lily hated more than being a third wheel was when her love life rose casually in a conversation. Lily frantically searched for a verbal detour to a different subject every time. "Busy with work, the Academy opening up and no time."

Desi gave her a doubtful look that bordered on judgment. Lily knew Desi meant well. It wasn't her friend's fault Lily's stance on not dating chafed. "Right. You know, I used similar excuses. Too busy. Too much work. Afraid to get my heart broken." She smiled with a laugh. "And Rez did a honey-do list I didn't write, but he did it anyway as if I did. That man would not go away."

Lily laughed, and the scene with the most recent man came to mind. Even with his good looks, she didn't consider Evan dating material. In fact, she didn't put any guy on that list. It was easy to keep track of with zero names on it. It also barred heartache. Lily's heart had broken once. It was not an endeavor she wished to survive a second time. "I'd love someone to hand off the annoying chores around the house. Bathe the dog. Pick up the poop in the yard. But then they would be at my house, and I have to deal with them not going away. I'd kick them in the nuts." She gave Desi a snarky smile. "Or practice my taser on them. A girl has to make sure her batteries work in all the things. I also have a battery-operated boyfriend that doesn't have nuts. But it also doesn't piss me off. It's better."

Desi laughed. "Girl, I wanted Rez to go and to kick him in the jewels too. But I'm glad I didn't. Those nuts came in handy later." She added a wicked wiggle of the brows.

"Whose nuts are you ladies discussing?"

Lily glanced behind her to find Beth Daniels-Bailey had been shopping and joined them. An athletically fit woman with hazel eyes and short black hair. A homicide detective with the San Francisco Police Department—one of its best. Beth married the hot, drool-worthy cowboy, ex-gunslinger William Jess Bailey—known by his family and friends as Jess. Immortal, over two centuries old, and to make relations even more colorful, the baby daddy of Lily's sister Emma's daughter Sophia. The one and same as Lily's boss at the Academy. "Well, for once, Beth, not your husband. But I'm pretty sure he would need a kick for something at some point." She laughed. "Maybe do it anyway to keep him in line."

Beth smiled as she shrugged. "We could do it and say it's credit for the next time he deserves one."

Lily laughed and introduced Beth to Desi. "Desi's man, Rez, used to work for the San Fran police. Maybe you knew him?"

"Rez Maine? Yeah, we ran in different divisions, but a righteous guy." Beth pointed her finger at Desi. "I heard he left the department for the Sunnyville force for a woman. Am I to presume you are her?"

Desi rolled her eyes, but it was easy to see that she took pride in the fact. "I am. But never say that in front of Rez. He thinks he's an alpha male and would never do anything as grand for a woman. I let him believe that most days."

Lily looked down at the bag Beth held to see infant supplies. "Are you shopping for little Mira?" Beth had been unable to carry a child to term, so she and Jess had recently adopted a baby girl. Lily knew they were trying to adopt a second child too. No other couple deserved children more than those two. Lily had no clue how the couple did it, both busy with their careers and Beth's mother combating Alzheimer's. The Baileys' hands were full. Lily happily settled on spoiling everyone else's children—or so she told herself anytime she spent time doing so.

"I am. She's constantly hungry like her father. That or Jess has begun craving baby formula because I seem to buy so much of the stuff. Or Mom." She screwed her face up. "God, I hope not. Mira's gas is disgusting enough from drinking it without adding Cowboy's to it."

Lily felt the same ache flare when talking to anyone about babies. Judging by Desi's expression, her friend felt the same. "Well, I need to get to work before your husband fires me, Beth." She turned to Desi and hugged her. "Call me, and we'll do dinner this week."

Desi nodded and looped her arm with Lily's. "I will. But you should find a date."

Beth walked with them. "I agree. There are some very eligible guys at work." Beth snapped her fingers. "Isn't Evan single? From what I hear, the guy could use a night out. Jess says the man is wound so tight he's driving everyone crazy."

Lily laughed at the thought. "Yeah, no. That is not going to happen. That man hates me." She smiled and added with a healthy level of snark. "And the feeling is mutual."

They made it to the door when two men suddenly rushed in. Both wore black clothes and masks.

But the most alarming part of their attire—guns held at the ready.

3

"Evan, we have a situation."

Typically, in a normal context, hearing such a statement was rare, but not in the Grid. Looking up from reading the reports, Evan raised a brow as the Relay burst into his office. "What type of situation?"

The man stepped in and held out a tablet.

Evan took the device, stood, and scrolled through the information listed on the screen. "A robbery gone wrong?" Not an uncommon crime in the city. "Why is that a concern to us?"

"They have hostages, and we have two people being held. The robbery took place at the grocery store on Fifth Street, the one acting as a front for our substation in the basement."

Evan's head shot up. Now the man received his full attention. "Please tell me it's not one of our locations with an armory?" The answer appeared on the man's face. No words were needed. "Fuck."

Evan rushed to the communications center within the deep underground facility. Three levels of reinforced walls containing an elaborate maze of tunnels. A bustling small city with its own airflow system, sewage, and water. A stock of military-grade weapons to rival any military base and a medical wing containing state-of-the-art equipment. Unknown to the human world under Fort Peace at the foot of the Golden Gate Bridge.

"Who do we have inside?" Evan barked as they moved.

"Beth Daniels and Lily Devenmore."

The names caused Evan's steps to falter and halt. A ball of dread dropped into his gut like a rock at the news. "Have we made Bailey aware his wife is there? Ms. Devenmore's family?" He fought to voice a question about injuries or fatalities. No, he didn't want to go there and left it unsaid. He knew the name causing his internal reaction—Lily Devenmore. Her condition should not matter more than Mrs. Bailey. Or anyone on the Grid. All were equal as resources under him.

The Relay nodded as they reached the busy communication hub in the center of the complex. "We made Bailey aware. We requested he not go to the scene. There's a large police response, and the press arrived as soon as it hit the scanner. We let Emma Sundown know her sister was there. In her pregnant state, Reno is keeping her at home."

"Let me guess, Cowboy didn't listen and went anyway?" He cut a sideways glance, splitting his attention for a moment from the large monitor screens mounted on the wall.

The Relay nodded. "Did you have to ask? Of course, he didn't. Does he ever?"

It was silly to ask. Both men's responses were no surprise to Evan. Cowboy was a throwback to another time when damsels in distress found themselves tied to railroad tracks waiting to be rescued by a cowboy gunslinger. One would think the man would have evolved over time, but that was not the case. The irony, Bailey's wife worked as one of the best police detectives in the city and was perfectly capable of defending herself. Perhaps two-hundred-year-old cowboys were the same as old dogs—incapable of learning new tricks.

Great, it wasn't even noon, and there would not be enough coffee to change the rest of the evening. "Get me there. Clear it with our connections within the police." He handed the Relay the tablet as he got his boots moving back to a run. "And let Bounce know. I'm taking point."

---

THE SHOUTING of male baritone voices indicated exactly where Evan needed to go on the scene. One held a deep southern Texas drawl. William Jess Bailey. The other, a clipped California accent—one Evan didn't recognize.

Crews isolated the section of the block surrounding the store with yellow crime scene tape. Police units parked crosswise on the streets to prevent any non-official vehicles intruding the secured space. Parked half in and out with tape across the bush guard was the cowboy's ridiculously large, black, lifted Ford truck. The vehicle was as unfit to live in the city as the man who drove it. Members of the press stood next to it, along with civilian spectators drawn to drama like flies. Many held up cameras and cell phones. Evan placed his hand up and kept his head down to stay out of camera shots. Uniformed police officers managed to keep the chaotic herd of humans and its containment under control.

Evan reached the area of raised voices to find Bailey bowed up to a man equal in height and size. Neither man gave the impression of backing down. Both were in full-blown alpha-male mode. If they had been peacocks, Evan was sure they would have had lovely plumage shaking during whatever type of a pissing contest a peacock could display. Both men blocked each other's entry to the police mobile command center set up in the center of the block. To the human eye, it appeared to be like any other reinforced trailer on wheels with a faded spot of graffiti on the bumper. To a member of Evan's world, it displayed a Grid emblem stating differently.

"I don't know who the hell you are, buddy. But my wife, a member of the San Fran po-po, is in there," Jess snarled as he jabbed a finger against the other man's chest, "so move out of my way." At *least* Jess hadn't shown fangs. Thank god for small favors. Yet judging by Bailey's bristling irritation, any minute now, that favor would be squashed. All Evan needed were more complications to the shit show than they had on their hands now.

"Well, I am a member of the Sunnyville Police force, former San Francisco SWAT, and my girlfriend is in there. So you move." The man then bumped chests with Jess, and fists were about to fly.

"Gentleman, calm down." Evan stepped between them to either defuse the situation or cause blows to land on him rather than the human. He hoped for the former, but it wouldn't be the first time he'd taken a hit from Bailey, nor him dishing out his own in response, but here was not the place. It was a fight and distraction Evan would like to avoid. "Let's discuss. You both have a reason for concern. But let's let the proper authorities handle this."

"No. Dammit, E. Beth is in there!" Jess said to him before directing his focus back to the other man. "And this fella just steps up and thinks he can ask for my damn credentials and even told *me* to get behind the damn tape like I'm a civi." Jess gave a smug smile. "Tell him he's wrong and send his ass on the other side with the yellow-taped day care folks."

The other man smirked. "Wrong, buddy. I'm not going anywhere. I'd like to see you pick me up to make me go."

"Enough!" Evan barked and placed a hand on each man's chest. "This is not helping the situation." Turning his back to Jess, he addressed the stranger. "I'm Evan O'Brien. I work with the San Francisco Police Department in a security consultant capacity. May I ask who you are? You said your girlfriend is inside? One of the hostages?"

"Consultant? Huh." The man's eyes scanned Evan in obvious doubt before he looked back up to meet his. "Reznor Maine. And yeah, my Desi is inside. And like I was telling Cowboy Woody here, former San Fran SWAT. I'm with the Sunnyville force now. We were in town for a convention."

"Disney insults is the best you can do?" Jess snorted. "See a string in my back, bud? Go ahead and try to find it. I dare you to try, asshole."

Evan would need an IV of coffee at this point. Screw the mug. Just tap a vein and give him the caffeine. "Bailey, I know it's tough for you to keep your mouth shut. But if you don't want to be put behind the tape, then shut up." He looked back over his shoulder and raised a brow. "And you know I *can* order that." Evan lowered his hands as he took a step back. "I must ask you both to wait here. Let me see what we can do to appease you both."

He stepped toward the command center and took a glance back. Both men still bristled with a testosterone-fueled need to protect a mate, but at least they were not throwing down—for now. It was a victory, albeit a delicate one. Evan didn't expect it to last for long.

Entering the interior of the trailer, he walked past the monitors and security panels that lined both sides. Men and women sat in front of the equipment—all of them were Relays, Grid's label for soldiers. Some worked for both it and the police department. The Grid, San Francisco's police force, and the city's government had worked together for decades, sharing both resources and secrets.

Evan reached the front, relieved to find that Miller, Detective Bailey's former partner, was the designated site commander. One less worry for Evan as Miller was a member of the Grid, and since they dealt with Grid property, a necessity. Speaking low, Evan motioned behind him toward the door. "I have Bailey outside. He's blowing a gasket because of Beth being inside. He's with a former SF SWAT member, a Reznor Maine. What do we know about him? He says his girlfriend, a woman by the name of Desi, is inside as well." He narrowed his eyes and crossed his arms. "I need to know if he's telling the truth, or they are a plant. The last thing I need is a demon playing dress-up as a human right now."

Miller tapped a man close-by who was wearing a headset. "Pull up a Reznor Maine's background. Police file. Anything you can find. See if he's legit."

As the communications officer performed the task, Miller

briefed Evan on what they did know. "The gunmen are two Caucasian males, mid-twenties to early thirties. They have locked the doors and shoved shelves in front of the two windows to block any view from a scope. There are five hostages in total from what we can register with the thermals. We sent a drone in through the trash chute, one they destroyed moments later." Miller lifted a printed paper from the console. "We pulled up traffic cams. They parked down the block from the store." Miller typed on a keyboard to bring up grainy video footage. "We grabbed a screenshot of their faces before they pulled down the masks. We then used facial recognition on the perps. Low-grade criminals. One on probation for two years for assault. His name is Charles Mathers. The other we have zero intel on. He's not in the system. Headquarters is still attempting to ID him."

Evan read through the details as Miller ran them down. "Did we learn of Beth and Lily's presence via their stamps?"

Miller gave him a nod for confirmation.

Evan bit his tongue to keep from asking if they were injured and paused to find their health status on the report. Nothing listed—good. Stamps were a moniker, resembling tattoos, given to all on the Grid. Stamps contained tiny nanobots that fed information on vital statistics and location back to HQ and were used for communication.

"Maine checks out, sir."

Both he and Miller turned to read the information about Reznor Maine on the monitor. His service records, driver's license, social security, down to date and place of birth. Everything the man said appeared to be true. A minor comfort to Evan. It wouldn't be the first time an enemy infiltrator intruded on a situation to make it worse for Grid's forces and to Hell's advantage. Evan stood upright to cross his arms and looked over at Miller. "His girlfriend is in there. And with his background, we have zero chance or reason to tell him to step off and let us handle this." He rubbed a hand on his forehead as he blew out a breath in frustration. "I can make the call to allow him knowledge of the Grid without Bounce's approval. But if proven wrong, the boss will hand me my ass in a brown paper bag."

Dropping his hand, he pointed to another monitor. "Have we been able to access the store's surveillance system?"

"Not yet, sir. It appears they disabled it," the Relay responded.

Evan braced his arms on the counter as he narrowed his eyes in thought. "What about the substation in the basement? Have they compromised it?"

The Relay pulled up the schematics for the building. "The entry is hidden behind this cooler against the back wall. They'd have no reason to know its existence or the entry point. It's not listed on any public records."

Well, that was a positive in this mess. Maybe they got lucky, and the two men were just hapless humans who had made bad choices. Crossing his arms, Evan swiveled his head to stare at the door where two pissed off males waited on the other side to be informed and included. He sympathized with both men. Each wanted to know how their females were. It was a safe bet, considering the background of Maine and the history of Bailey, neither would settle for an update and wait for news. No amount of Evan wishing would likely keep them out of his way.

As Evan considered the various options to proceed, Maine's background in SWAT could be of value to the operation, and Bailey had served as a mediator in heated situations in the past.

"Get me a copy of our NDA."

# 4

$\mathscr{L}$ ily had three things on her shopping list. Granola bars, frozen organic pizza rolls, and dog treats. She purchased the items with no problem. The dog treats were even a buy one, get one free—yay for her. Not on the list? The two armed idiots holding the store up. The thrill of her BOGO was ruined. Lily doubted they expected the police to arrive so quickly. They either planned for it just in case or adapted well on the fly.

The hostages were led to the back of the store in the small frozen goods section. One man kept his gun trained on the five of them while the other blocked the front windows using rolling shelves from the registers. They disabled the cameras in the store, and the hub of the security system was thrown to the floor hard enough to illicit sparks. With that, the robbery became a hostage standoff with police.

Lily sat between Desi and Beth. She tracked the two idiot criminals as they paced and spoke to each other, not loud enough for Lily to hear what they were saying. She leaned to the right to whisper to Beth. "Are you armed? Have a weapon?"

Beth kept her eyes forward to observe the two men as she replied, "No. Off duty and left it in the glove box of my car. Same with the shield."

While that sucked, Lily felt a little relieved. The last thing they needed was for those two men to learn a cop existed among the hostages. She glanced over at Desi and smiled slightly. Desi occupied herself by checking her nails and appeared nonplussed. Lily knew better. Her friend's foot swung side to side nervously. Desi once told her about some pervert who broke into her home. The perv had a creepy habit of standing at the end of women's beds to watch them sleep. But Desi put a positive spin on that horror—it played a part in Rez coming into her life. While that worked great for Desi and her man, it was not one Lily cared to try. Until GrubHub allowed men to be delivered, and Lily could customize to her tastes, love was not on the menu. The thought of food delivery caused her stomach to grumble. Teach her to consider a Starbucks latte as lunch. She reached into her bag of groceries and dug around for a snack. Yes, she ate her feelings, and this situation held a boatload of emotions. Finding a granola bar, she regretted not buying a Snickers bar, a Kit-Kat, some Ben and Jerry's—but she had, once again, for the billionth time in her life, decided to diet.

*Picked a shitty day to start that, Lily.* But in her defense, was there a suitable day to give up chocolate? Really? Lily didn't think so.

Guessing the two men were attempting to form a plan, her head went down to eat the bar when the stamp on the inside of her wrist buzzed. Out of the corner of her eye, Lily saw Beth discreetly reach up to touch hers located on her collar bone. Their two eyes met for a moment—Grid knew the situation and that they were being held. Help must be on the way, if not already on site.

"Excuse me!" Lily threw a hand up in the air and called out to the thugs. When they both turned to look at her, she put on her biggest, brightest smile. "I need to potty."

The two men stared at her like they did not understand such a basic bodily function. She knew they spoke English. And surely they took a piss occasionally. "Pee. I need to pee. And I'd like not to do it sitting here." She fluttered her eyelashes and coated her tone with verbal honey. "I'd appreciate it so much if I could go to the restroom."

The two men conversed, and one stepped over to her. "Fine, get up."

Lily held a hand up for assistance and received a snort instead. And no help—rude. So much for utilizing the tactic to slam the guy's head into the glass-doored freezer behind her. Maybe they were smarter than she thought. And not as dumb as she had hoped.

Smirking, she stood and waggled a finger at his gun. "If you shoot me for needing to pee, I will be pissed in another way."

The man lowered it and then shoved her toward the bathroom with his free hand. "Move."

The distance to the ladies' room was a short one—only ten steps. As the man pushed the door open, he ordered Lily to stay outside in the hall. Lily watched him check it for escape, something she had hoped for. *Please have a window.*

Unfortunately, it didn't, and she hid her disappointment. It only had cheerfully painted pink concrete walls, two stalls, and a single sink. When he motioned for her to enter, Lily did a mock curtsey but found a boot wedged at the bottom of the door when she tried to close it.

"Leave it open."

Lily crossed her arms over her chest and twisted her lips. "Are you kidding me? I can't do that. I have a bashful bladder. If it knows you're standing right there, listening for whatever weird reason you have for witnessing my piss, I won't be able to relieve myself. And we're both going to be spending all day waiting for me to pee." She lifted her shoulders with a shrug, "I'm up for that if you are. But I'll be sitting down. You'll be standing there looking like a weirdo." She leaned against the doorway. "Choice is yours. What'll it be?" Her broad smile returned with a heap of smugness.

The man shoved his skimask up in irritation and regarded her.

"Funny, you said you could piss out there, sitting with everyone to see. Suddenly you lose the ability to do just that?"

Lily rolled her eyes. "That was sarcasm out there. It's a coping mechanism when faced with being held hostage by two armed men. Or are you unable to tell when someone is being a smartass?" She let out a laugh. "Ah, honey, you will get schooled the longer I'm here. It'll be fun for both of us."

The man gave her a scathing smirk and moved his boot. "Make it quick. And no fucking tricks."

Lily laughed. "Tricks? In a bathroom? What are you expecting me to do exactly? Paper dolls out of toilet tissue?" She stepped inside and called back as the door closed. "Not one of my talents, sorry."

The moment she was alone, she rushed to the farthest stall and threw the lock to secure it. Touching her stamp, she felt the light sensation of electricity, causing the hair on her arm to stand as it went online on her end. Bringing her wrist up a few inches from her mouth, she whispered, "Hello, it's Lily. Is anyone there?"

## 5

"*L*et me get this straight. Are you telling me you two are immortal? That you are some secret supernatural army? And you want me to sign this"—Reznor's gaze swung down to read the paper in his hand a second time—"nondisclosure agreement stating clearly in paragraph three, if I speak of it, I risk, what?" He smirked. "Severe and life-altering consequences?" He nailed both Evan and Jess with a disbelieving, threatening glare. "Is that legal-speak for dropping my ass in the bay?"

Jess stepped up into Rez's personal space. "I can make that happen, bud. In fact…" He gave a deadly smile. "I'll most likely enjoy it enough to do a little two-step on the bridge as your body hits the water."

Evan closed his eyes and rubbed a hand over his face. He felt like he was babysitting the brawniest, deadliest toddlers on the planet. He couldn't blame either man—their women were inside and being held by armed men with one possibly injured. Headquarters monitored both Beth and Lily's vitals, but Maine's girlfriend had no such technology. "Stop it. Both of you."

He found himself once again between the two men and addressed Jess first. "Put away the 'my dick is bigger than yours' mentality, Cowboy. Or I'll ask you to leave the scene." He gave the man a stern look and a creased brow. "And I will lock you out of the systems, including your stamp. Is that what you want? Because I can make it happen in a snap."

"This is bullshit, and you know it, E," Bailey spat in response but did as Evan requested as he leaned against the counter.

Focusing on Maine, Evan assessed where the man stood on learning about their world. He appeared skeptical but perhaps not dismissing it as fantasy, either. "What you stated is correct. And we've kept this secret for centuries. If you'd like me to call the deputy mayor and the police chief to verify who and what we are, I can. However, is that time we care to waste?"

He tapped the NDA held in Maine's hand. "Sign it. Help us deescalate this current situation and go about your life—without ever discussing anything you've seen or learned here. It's that simple." Evan softened his tone to gain Maine's trust to some level. "We have technology found only in a SWAT member's wet dreams. We can get your girlfriend and our people out of there. It's a matter of you helping us or not." He met the man's eyes. "It's your choice. Sign and stay. Or don't sign and go." He pushed the man's hand to press the document against Maine's chest. "Sign it. We could use your help."

Reznor opened his mouth and went fish-faced, possibly to utter more protests and doubts. But then he turned with the NDA, picked up a pen, and signed it. "Fine. I'll help your science fiction army. Whatever it takes to get my girl."

---

"HELLO, it's Lily. Is anyone there?" Lily's whispered voice came over the speaker in the trailer, routed via headquarters from her stamp.

Evan braced his hands on the counter with the microphone to answer her. "We hear you, Ms. Devenmore. Are you well? The others? Can you tell us about the persons in charge of your containment?" Bailey and Maine joined him, the two men standing on the left and right.

"Are you serious?"

Evan frowned in confusion and keyed the mic back on to reply. "Quite serious as this is a dire situation, Ms. Devenmore. Are you hurt? Are the other—"

"Stop, Evan. Lily. I'm being held as a hostage by idiots with guns. *Surely* you can call me Lily for this? You *can't* be that much of an asshole."

Jess let out a snort with a chuckle and crossed arms on his chest. "Oh, yeah, that's Lily. She could bleed out and still find her snark. It's a Devenmore trait. Runs through the whole bloodline." He sighed. "Sophia ain't even a teenager, and I already see that side from her mama."

Squeezing his eyes shut to hold his irritation at both Devenmore and Bailey, Evan counted to a silent five and keyed the microphone again. "Fine. Lily. What can you tell us about the hostages? The two men holding you. Are there any injuries?"

There was a lengthy pause, and for a moment, Evan thought the connection had dropped.

"They don't seem like total idiots, but it looks like they planned for an easy robbery and escape more than the current mess. And everyone is fine. They hurt no one. Beth is here, but she doesn't have her gun or a badge. Which is good—"

There was a sound of banging, like a fist on a door, from Lily's end. Jess pushed Evan to the side to speak into the microphone. "Lily, darlin'. I need you to tell Beth I'm here. And I'm going to get you all out and make those two men pay for ruining our damn evening."

Evan reached to move Bailey out of his way, but Maine prevented Evan from doing the job first. "Hey, ma'am. It's Lily, right? This is Reznor Maine. I'm Desi's boyfriend. Is she okay?" Maine turned his head to give Bailey a shit-eating smile. "Tell her I'm here. And if Cowboy Woody would get out of my way, I will see her soon for you and me to meet finally."

"This again? Gentlemen, just stop." Evan shoved them both from the microphone. "Lily, hang tight." He went to say more, but a slamming sound filled the airway, followed by an angry-sounding male voice. And the link disconnected.

"Dammit," Evan mumbled under his breath. Looking sideways at Bailey, he saw the same concern mirrored on Bailey's face. If Lily went offline, they could only hope she didn't get caught, not only compromising Grid technology but the men hurting her.

Or worse yet—he turned from the console, the rock feeling in his stomach growing—the link ended because they killed her. And more deaths might follow.

6

"**G**et off me!"

Idiot #2, as Lily called the underling of this stunt, burst into the bathroom. He kicked the door of the stall open just as she flushed the toilet for effect. He grabbed her stamped wrist, disconnecting the link to the Grid, as he hauled her out of the bathroom.

He pushed her toward the others, and she moved to #2, putting a pointed finger against his chest. "That is no way to handle a lady. You better be glad I wasn't doing number two, #2." The guy gave her a sneer and pushed her down to sit in the same spot as before. Dropping next to Beth, she couldn't help but see the amusement on both her and Desi's face. She mumbled, "Even big, bold women," then raised her voice to yell at the men, "deserve some manners!"

Idiot #1, now without his mask, came over to squat in front of her. Taking her chin in his fingers roughly, he came in too close for Lily's liking. "I'm tempted to shoot you so that I don't have to hear your mouth run. I'd advise you to use *your* manners so I don't have to. Clear?"

So, Idiot #1 might be smarter than the other one. Lily found raw intelligence reflected in his eyes to solidify that estimation.

Meeting his gaze as intensely, she nodded. "Fine. Then tell your minion to leave a girl alone when she's taking care of business." She smiled. "Please."

The man pulled a fist back to hit her, but Lily refused to flinch as she braced for the blow.

"Charlie, don't, man."

Idiot #2 grabbed the man's wrist, and now Lily knew his name. Charlie stood and stepped away. "Fine, but if the bitch keeps mouthing off, I'll stop her from doing it." He glanced back at Lily with a deadly expression. "We only need two hostages to get our point across, Kyle. Mouthy ones are expendable." The two men moved away toward the front of the store.

*Charlie and Kyle. Noted.* Left alone, Lily leaned into Beth and whispered, "Evan and Jess are outside." She reached over and took Desi's hand as she pressed closer to her. "Reznor is here too. With them." She let out soft snort. "And from the sounds of it, Evan has his hands full with the cowboy and Reznor. They both pulled the alpha cards save my woman card."

Desi sharply shifted her gaze to the front of the store. "Oh, lord. He is such a moron. That man will get himself killed. And yet, that's so encouraging." She closed her eyes and squeezed Lily's hand. "That means this will end soon, right?"

"Sounds like your man and mine will be besties or butting heads until they knock each other out." Beth was pissed. "And he better not die. Not—" But she snapped her mouth shut.

*Again,* Lily thought, and she knew why. Jess had already died once in the Old West. Then a second time more recently because of strange circumstances even for the Grid. The expressions of both concern and pride on her two friends' faces spoke of two women deeply in love. Lily didn't have to fall into that category to recognize it. Her sister Emma wore it every time her husband, Reno, went off to patrol.

"I think Evan is running point. Or so it seems." Lily snorted and dug around for another granola bar and held more out for everyone. "He will not rush in here like a knight on a white horse." She bit into the bar after unwrapping it. "The stick in his ass makes riding a horse painfully impossible."

She tracked one of the two men as he approached. He kept darting glances back over his shoulder when he arrived. "You want sodas?" He pointed to the coolers the hostages sat against. "Chips or something?" He opened one of the coolers at the end and pulled out five bottles of pop. "There's Sprite. I like Dr. Pepper myself."

He squatted down in front of Beth and Lily, his focus skipping randomly to the other man. "Look, we didn't mean for this to happen. I'm sorry, okay?"

Lily took a Sprite and cracked it open. "What did you think would happen if you held up a store? While it's open? With people in it?" She took a big drink. "Not to mention an organic food store? Who does that? That's the lamest robbery in the history of Darwin awards."

"She's right. You two guys will win first place," Desi added with a snort as she took a bottle of soda.

"Ladies. Let's not poke the bear armed with a gun." Beth leaned forward to say quietly to him. "Look, I understand how this went wrong. But you can end it." She glanced at the elderly shop owners. "They aren't well. This is stressful. And the more time that ticks by, the worse this is going to become. Give up, walk out, and we can all deal with the fallout."

The guy sat back on his haunches. He wrapped his arms around himself, rocked and shook his head. "No. You don't fucking understand." He snorted. "Wearing your nice clothes, spending way too much money on organic food. It's no different. You know that, right? Just a gimmick to make bougie women like you pay higher prices."

He swallowed, and Lily watched him scratch at his arms. Cutting a sideways glance at Beth, she could tell the detective had noticed it too. Drugs. Or the guy's nerves were frayed from stress.

"Fine. You're right. We don't get it. We've never been in such a spot to rob a store. Or threaten innocent people. Make an old couple scared." Yeah, Lily knew she might be pushing the guy a bit too far, even without Beth's warning tap on her arm. Frustration had a way of dissolving filters. Not that she had one, to begin with.

He rocked forward and grabbed Lily's arm. "Are you judging me? Should I remind you I'm the one with the gun? Maybe you need to listen to your friend."

Lily hissed as the man's fingers dug into her arm but held their visual lock. "But I can tell you this. I work with kids. And I know how to recognize a wounded, scared kid. While you may be an adult, inside, we all have inner children. And yours is frightened. Who wouldn't be? Look outside at all those cops. All they want to do is end this. One way or another."

Lily brought her hand up to lay over his, and her voice softened. "I don't know you. At all. In any other circumstance in this city, we never would. But the way I look at it, we're in this together. Maybe opposing sides, but still together." She pressed her lips together. She felt sorry for the guy. It wasn't difficult to see he never wanted to be in this mess. "I will help you end this in some way that gets us all out of here. But my friend is correct. The longer this goes on, the harder it's going to be to turn back." She sighed. "And when a situation gets to a certain boiling point, it's impossible to cool it down."

"Listen to her. She's right. You know she is," Beth added in a whisper.

The man darted his eyes around. "I don't know. I just—"

Jerked back suddenly, Charlie pointed a gun at them. He swung it wide with a snarl. "What the fuck is going on back here?" He pivoted to kick Kyle. "I told you not to talk to them. Why don't you ever listen?"

The other man scurried away, and she adjusted her attention to Charlie—no question who was in charge. "Nothing is going on. Other than you being a bully. We were thirsty. I asked for a soda, and he was kind enough to get it for us." She smiled. "He was being polite. Maybe you should try it. I hear it's good for the soul."

The man swung the gun up, most likely to hit her with it. Kyle wasn't close enough to stop the second attempt. Lily remained steadfast and calm. "Hurt a hostage. Do it, and see how well things go for you. I asked for a soda." She lifted her chin in defiance. "He helped. Nothing is going on. So why don't you just calm down? I'm cranky. I'm sorry. I'll sit here and be a good little hostage. Okay?"

The leader looked doubtful for a few seconds that she'd be able to pull it off before he stood to pull the other man away. She let out a held breath as they reached the middle of the store.

"That was either smart or stupid, Lily," Beth whispered with a sideways glance.

Lily brought a hand up to rub her forehead, where a headache began to bloom. *Great, wonder which aisle Tylenol is located?* Could she reach it from there? And her ass was going to sleep. "A little of both. I learned that there are two types of bullies. One that backs up what is said by doing. And one that is all talk and no do." Her head dropped back to rest against the cool glass of the cooler. "Interesting that we have both types. Kyle is no bully at all. All talk. Scared. Of the situation and what might happen at the end of all this."

Beth nodded. "And Charlie, calling all the shots, is all bully who backs up what he says without much thought or control. He would hit you. Of that, I have no doubt. Good job not reacting." She smiled and squeezed a hand on Lily's thigh. "You'd make a good cop."

Lily chuckled. "Running a school is about the same thing." She rolled her head to regard Beth. "Just the cutest criminals you'd ever want to meet."

EVAN SAT in the control center as he drank his sixth, seventh coffee? Not sure. But either way, no plans to leave and get shut-eye. His eyes went to the digital clock mounted above the monitors. They had three hours before dawn, and when that hit, he'd become isolated inside of the trailer until dusk. Time was running out fast. They now had a blueprint and layout of the store and the basement beneath it. As he ran his fingers along the lines etched on the paper, an idea spawned. A reckless one, but he couldn't get the thoughts of possible causes of Lily's loss of transmission out of his head. It ate at him, not knowing. *If those bastards harm her...* Imagining the ways and things they could have done to her made Evan begin to seethe with rage. At the thought that they dared to touch her, it bubbled through widening cracks in his hardened control. Dead. It made zero fucking sense. He'd have to figure out the misplaced emotions later. For now, he didn't need to know.

"Maine, do you have hostage negotiation training?"

The man glanced Evan's way from where he rested against a counter. "Yeah, most SWAT members take the courses at one point or another. What are you thinking?"

*I think I want those sons of bitches dead,* Evan thought. "We need to get in there. For obvious reasons, our time is limited. Those two may not know it, but they are on top of an arsenal and enough technology to start a small terrorist group. I have very little assurance that those two are random civilian criminals. Add to that?" His focus slid to the clock and then over to Bailey. "We now have a little more than two hours to end this."

"Evan, I hear you and all. But buddy, have you forgotten that you can't exactly, well, get a tan?" Jess walked over and picked up the schematics. "And this place is nothing but a big ole tanning bed when the sun comes up with all these windows." He frowned for a moment, and his eyes went wide. "There's a blur point in the basement. You cannot be thinkin' to use that?" He snorted. "It's ancient. We ain't got no idea if it even works. Or, if it does, and it's not calibrated, your ass ends up in the center of China Town in broad daylight."

"Hold up." Maine joined them. "How about we dumb that down to a level that isn't some blockbuster superhero movie bullshit. What does the sun have to do with any of this? And what is a blur point?"

Evan rubbed a hand over his face and addressed Maine first. Odd that answering his questions was the easiest path to travel down. "A blur point is between A and B. A is where you are. B is where you want to go. Our stamps make it a matter of being at the first and thinking and arriving at the second. In human terms, it's teleportation."

Jess's finger tapped on a circle within another on the paper. "In our facilities, we isolate where personnel comes and goes. Some of the demons and members of the opposing army have manifestation capabilities. No one wants to have their day interrupted by ugly mofos stealing the fresh doughnuts." He snorted. "See, we ain't so different. Cops like doughnuts. Badasses like them too."

"Cops are *badasses* too, Woody," Maine mumbled as his jaw tensed. "Teleportation. Demons. Still weird shit." He cleared his throat. "I'm starting to see the need for signing an NDA. That's next level." He crossed his arms and scrutinized the layout. "So, you can't use that tech in the daytime?"

Jess snorted. "Oh, sure we can—once we retire, and Hell gives us a gold coin. Free to live as good citizens who happen to live forever. But Evan ain't done that yet, and it means he goes all crispy in the sun. A big ole handsome pork skin. Crunchy and baked but smells a hell of a lot worse." Jess tapped his fangs. "These are for predators. And also a little gift from Hell so we never, ever forget who could pull our strings on a whim. And dark things, while allowed to go bump in the night, go crispy during the light of day. The last thing we want is that. I ain't had it happen personally, but I have a pretty creative imagination. Ain't something I'd care to get first-hand knowledge of."

Maine stared at Bailey. Disbelief crystal clear on the man's features. "Like vampires? And Hell? Dark? I thought you were the good guys? Color me confused."

"No. We are not vampires. We're different. The fangs and sun are the only things we have in common," Evan responded with his head back in frustration. "And this quick education is wasting time we do not have." His nostrils flared with an exhale. "A summary will have to do. We once all were wicked. Criminals, murderers. The dredge of humanity. We even had Jack the Ripper on our team until he reverted his ways and got bounced back to Hell. Bailey was a gunslinger. I was the right-hand man for the mob in the twenties. But we've been given a second chance to leave Hell and redeem our pasts. So yes, we are the good guys—now. We just spent a little time with the devil before getting our redemption ticket."

Maine appeared as baffled as before but ceased with the questions. "Fine. Blurring is some *Star Trek* shit. And sunlight is not your friend. Let's move on to the plan. And how does my having negotiating skills play into it?"

Evan ran his tongue along the inside of his cheek, avoiding the temptation to look at the clock again. Not that it would stop the passage of time, but it would add unwanted logic into the calculations of the plan. Logic, for once, needed to step back. "I want to use that blur point, come up through the basement, get the back door open, and then get the hostages out of there. And take those two out. Not necessarily kill them, but be aware it's a potential outcome."

"Perhaps you don't understand what the word *negotiation* means." Maine put a hand on his chest. "Or my world is unaware of your definition. Here it means you de-escalate a situation—to prevent death or a violent end. Your definition sounds very clearly the opposite of that."

"What he's sayin' is this." Jess leaned against a counter, crossing his arms and ankles with his head downcast. "If these two fellas are from your world, then we'll do our best to save them. We ain't allowed to kill innocent humans. But if they aren't and are from our world *or* a threat to it, that's a game-changer."

Bailey pushed off to stand in front of Maine. "As I said, our two worlds ain't so different. My wife is a cop, and we both know it's a hard job with life and death decisions—with both good and bad, in all the aspects. The only difference here is you might have a sniper on a rooftop to eliminate the threat in situations." He turned his head to meet Evan's level gaze with one of his own. "Whereas, we are the rifle. And we are also the scope and the bullet."

"You sure of this, E?"

Evan wore full tactical gear with a Velcro strip designating him as San Francisco police. The Grid often did the latter to blend into police operations and cooperative takedowns. Bailey checked the straps like a mother hen, and Evan smacked his hands away. "Yes. I'm the only one for this. You have children and your wife, Beth, in the store. You are emotionally entangled. The same applies to Maine."

"We're ready, Evan."

Both him and Jess looked over at the Relay. Maine's role was simple but could also become complicated fast if this went sideways. He had to get the hostages and the two men holding them to the front of the store, using negotiation to show each hostage was alive and unharmed before discussing any demands. Evan, at the same time, would utilize the blur point in the basement, enter the establishment, and unlock the rear door. Maine would then manipulate the two criminals to remain in front with discussions, and then carefully con the two gunmen to return the hostages to the rear of the store. The key lay in using the landline at the front of the store at the manager's desk. In discussion and planning, it all seemed efficient and easy.

But after a century on the Grid, Evan knew any type of plan, regardless of its difficulty level of execution, risked going south. The easy ones traversed there faster than the complicated ones. Murphy's law in warfare.

Maine stood ready with the communications Relay, who instructed him on how to use the special communication setup and headset to tap into the store's telephone system. They needed any calls routed to the one phone in the store's front rather than across the switchboard. It took time, and now Evan had less than an hour to get the job done. Rolling his head on his neck, followed by loosening up his shoulders and arms, he gave a nod. HQ triangulated the coordinates of the blur point to his stamp, and he closed his eyes.

As he vanished, he heard the other two men.

"Holy shit," Maine stated in a voice full of awe.

Jess grinned. "Told you. We're cool like that and have the best toys."

IN THE FEW seconds it took for Evan to blur from the command trailer, he performed the fastest prayer in the history of praying that he didn't have the potential outcome Bailey had suggested.

With the restructuring of his cells completed, he found himself surrounded by pitch-black darkness. Placing his hand on his service weapon, he touched the stamp placed on his hip bone.

"I'm in. Can you confirm?"

"Confirmed, sir. We show your coordinates directly under the store in our substation. Booting up the systems under black op protocol," the Relay replied.

Panels of controls came to life with a hum, too low of a level to be heard above the bunker. A dim green light over his head blinked on, and he could see his surroundings. A heavy coat of dust layered everything. The stench of stale air was thick as the systems came online. All substations were constructed with a closed, recirculating filtered air system. When it kicked in, it stirred the dust, causing it to dance in the thick air. A cot sat at one end next to an open bathroom with a shower, commode, and sink. Above the two monitors and keyboards, a secured shelf on the wall held bottled water and MREs. Pulling one down, Evan wiped the dust off the packaging to find the expiration date drew near within a few months.

"Yum," he mumbled in disgust. He should have brought a pizza or two.

*Wonder what kind she likes?*

Cursing at letting his mind waste time on such petty thoughts, he moved around the bunker to get an idea of the actual layout. He knew from the building layout a locked door in the ceiling led to a tube with a rung ladder to access the ground floor of the store above. Then, it would be a matter of sliding the cooler or tracks to the side once Maine performed his tasks, and the plan would be done.

"Easy cheesy, lemon squeezy," he whispered.

The line of communication remained open, and he reached up to find the keypad on the door above. "What's the code for the substation door?" He needed to ensure it still functioned. He would have zero time to waste, trying to override it. Shooting his gun at it would be useless. The door was made with ballistic and blast reinforced steel. All substation entries were. And it was the only way in or out of the space. Receiving the code, Evan entered it, and the lock popped with a dull thud.

Now to wait.

---

Lily's stamp buzzed at the same time a landline phone rang at the front of the store. She dared a look at Beth and then Desi. She strained to overhear the conversation after Charlie answered the call. Unable to and the effort making her headache pound, she closed her eyes. *Please be the end of this.* The bad guys in movies asked for a pizza, a helicopter, a million dollars, or lifetime passes to Disney World. No matter the demand, she wanted it met in order to go home to her pup and pull the Ben & Jerry's Chunky Monkey from her freezer. She'd put this behind her and resolve, once again, to start her diet tomorrow—after she finished her ice cream, of course.

Without warning, Kyle rushed to the five of them and yelled for them to get to their feet. After helping the elderly shop owner to his feet, with Desi assisting the man's wife, Lily followed everyone else to the front of the store. Able to see over the shelves, Lily whistled in awe at the scene of activity outside. Dozens of police cars and armored vehicles with flashers on—glaring even in the pre-dawn light. She scanned through the clutter of the force until her gaze landed on the matte black painted trailer parked behind the other vehicles—a mobile command center. Lily couldn't see the bumpers, but judging by the lack of branding, the Grid controlled the scene. Beth took Lily's hand and gave a squeeze. The lady cop must have looked for it too, and Lily assumed it offered the same relief to her.

"You see them, right? We haven't hurt them at all," Charlie stated in a tense, angry tone to whoever spoke on the opposite end of the phone call. "We just wanted the money. And that's all we want now. Back off, get us a car, and we're out of here. You can have the hostages. We never planned to have any. But we are not going to just fucking give up."

Kyle hung back, chewing on a nail, and nervously paced. "Tell them we ain't going to hurt them. I don't want to hurt anyone, Charlie. Tell them." He grabbed the other man's arm. "I don't want to get sniped! Tell them we aren't going to hurt them!"

Charlie shoved the man back, glaring at him. He covered the mouthpiece of the phone to hiss. "Are you an idiot? We tell them that, and we lose our bargaining power. Just shut up and let me do this, okay, little brother?"

*Brothers. Were they brothers?* With that new knowledge, she could see the resemblance. That complicated things a bit—loyalty ran deeper with a brother than it did for a fellow crook.

Charlie returned to the call as he turned to face Lily and the others. "Go back to where you were." He hurriedly waved a hand toward them as he turned his back and remained on the call. Kyle backed that command with a half-assed wave of this gun but stayed with his brother to listen in on the negotiations.

Doing as they were told, the group made it to the back of the store. Then a whispered voice came from Lily's stamp. Beth tensed at her side to indicate she received the same.

"I need you to get the hostages to me. By the hall to the bathrooms."

Lily frowned in confusion, and she leaned forward enough to find Evan stood in the darkness of that hallway. "What the—" she whispered before snapping her mouth shut. Her gaze swung to the front of the store. The two men still faced the windows, engaged on the call. Beth nodded, and Lily was glad to have company within the sudden insanity.

She checked a second time to make sure Charlie and Kyle remained busy before she stood up slowly and put a finger against her lips to keep the others quiet. Once again helping the elderly couple up, they held hands to form a chain and move. Staying low, hoping the rows of goods on the shelves gave them cover, they shuffled as quietly as possible to the hall. Evan took the older couple first. Beyond him, Lily could see both Jess and another equally tall, broad man next to him at the open back door. Must be Reznor Maine. Lily recognized him from Desi's social media. Both men were attired in heavy tactical gear and took the couple to help exit the store.

As the three moved from the opening of the store, Lily saw the danger of the escape diminish by the fact the morning touched the sky. Her eyes locked with Evan's. Why did he take this kind of chance? Was he insane? Was he remaining behind? How did he get here? Questions flew through her mind at a frantic pace. She worried her headache might erupt into a stroke.

Evan gave her a clipped nod at her apparent alarm—the stark reality of the danger he placed himself impossible to hide. Lily never considered Evan to be the hero type. That designation involved allowing some level of chaos occasionally. Evan clung obsessively tight to control. Strange considering he had been a fighter decades before being placed in the level of command he was in now. She never considered him in any other role.

Beth hung back to monitor the two men in front. Desi was the next to exit, and Reznor's eyes brightened at seeing her, but otherwise, he restrained his reaction at seeing his love. Desi caressed his cheek quickly as she passed to disappear from view. Only she and Beth remained.

Moving toward the exit, Lily paused in front of Evan after Beth reached her cowboy. "What are you doing?" Lily hissed in a baffled whisper through her teeth. "You can't go out there now. It's daytime."

Evan grasped her arm. "I have an exit plan. But first, I need you out of here." He pulled her firmly toward the door. "Just go, please."

Lily's mouth opened to protest, but without warning, shots rang out. Evan angled his body to block her from the line of fire as they were forced toward the bathrooms, sparing Lily from the bullet that struck the brick wall an inch from her head. Charlie and Kyle ran toward them, firing their weapons as they advanced. The back door slammed shut as Kyle reached it while Charlie advanced on her and Evan. Lilly yelped in alarm when Evan took her hand and returned fire to buy some cover to vacate the hall. Glass on the coolers shattered, spraying them both with shards as they passed. Sodas burst to spray as bullets struck.

They reached the last of the coolers, and Evan grabbed its handle as he continued to fire behind them.

"You want a soda now?" Lily yelled in flustered disbelief. But then the thing slid to the side, and rather than a wall, a dark opening yawned behind it. A shot burst a gallon of milk right next to them, and Evan moved her behind him.

"Go!"

Lily felt him jerk against her and heard him let out a grunt. Blood spread on his shoulder and arm to the side of the vest. More shots rang out, and Evan shoved her into the opening behind the cooler. She hit a wall, barely avoiding falling down a tunnel in the floor.

"Move! Now!"

Lily didn't have to be told twice. More shots hit the space, thudding into the concrete walls, ricocheting off a large metal door down into the space below. She heard the cooler slide back in place and muffled the shots from above. Hitting the floor, she looked up to see Evan rushing down the rungs. He slammed the door above the tunnel, and it came down with a solid clang. He threw a heavy-duty bolt when, seconds later, pings bounced off the door. Most likely, the two criminals were attempting to breach it with gunfire.

Lily took a second to look around her before whipping around to glare at Evan. "This was *your* plan? To go crispy? To—" But her words cut off when Evan collapsed to the floor.

8

*E*van felt the most incredible warmth and softness. He sought more of it. He turned toward the source of such heat and let out a sigh. It was nice—so fucking nice—and he wondered if a one-night stand may have spent the night. He usually didn't allow it. He couldn't recall the last time he cuddled another person.

When his brain snapped awake to bring with it the memory of the latest events and who he must be cuddling, he opened his eyes to find Lily Devenmore against him. At first, he thought her unconscious until a soft snore told him differently. They lay on one of the cot mattresses moved to the floor. Frowning and disoriented, he discovered his vest removed along with his shirt. A large bandage was taped to his shoulder. Judging by the pain, he'd taken a hit during the firefight.

Lifting carefully to rest on his elbow, he checked Lily visually for injury from the flying bullets and debris. Her dark, wavy hair now loosened from her ponytail, he gently moved it from her face with a light touch. He wanted her to sleep—humans required rest, and undoubtedly, she must be exhausted after the ordeal. She let out a soft moan and cuddled closer. He froze as he let her resettle. Finding no sign of blood on her clothes, he trailed his attention from her ebony hair, down her shirt, jeans, and landing on her feet in sneakers. Reversing the examination, he skimmed to her hips and paused—plump, lush and rounded. Evan caught a glimpse of the slight cresting of her ass. He already knew that it, too, shared the attribute of her hips. He had watched it more than he would care to admit. Whenever they argued, she deliberately showed it to him with her slapping a cheek as she walked away. Usually, with a specific finger held up in the air to complete the picture, considering herself the victor—or refusing to admit defeat.

As his admiring view reached her stomach, he was delighted to find her shirt rode up to expose bare, creamy skin. He fixated on her belly button and the soft area around it. It looked… *Fuck…* well, comfortable. Evan never took time in his quick, frantic sexual trysts to consider how sexy a woman's torso could be. Lily made him regret many missed opportunities of doing so with others before. He wondered what it would be like to rest his head there, to lick that belly button. Would she be ticklish under his tongue? Or would she squirm with the promise he'd lick else-where? To have her long fingers run through his hair. Combing and stroking, nails scraping his scalp. *Stroking more than just his hair—*

"E?"

Her voice hauled him out of those sinful musings with a start, and his eyes lifted to find hers. She looked drowsy. A heavy weariness showed in their green depths.

He sat up and grimaced slightly in pain. "Are you injured, Ms. Devenmore?"

"Seriously?"

She said the singular word and swung a fist to strike him in the chest. The impact reverberated through the shoulder injury, and he hissed. It took no genius to guess the reason behind the blow's delivery.

"I'm sorry. Are you injured?" He turned his head to regard her. "Lily?"

"See, not difficult at all. Thank you." She lifted off the mattress and sat across from him. "I'm not the one that got a new hole, Evan," Lily said as she touched the bandage on his shoulder. "I found an exit wound, so that's good. But it bled big time. I put a few stitches in it." She brought her eyes to his, and Evan felt a strange thrill to see the level of concern in her gaze. "I can't believe you passed out getting shot only once. Wuss."

Ah, so much for that tender moment.

"I also have not slept nor eaten in over twenty-four hours." He shot a smirk in her direction. "I have been busy trying to rescue certain persons." He reached up to touch his skull and found a decent-sized lump. "And I struck my head trying to move one of those certain persons out of the way of that one shot." He rose to stand. "You are welcome, by the way."

Lily sputtered and jumped to her feet. "So *that* was your plan? That sucked as far as plans go! Are we free? No. Did you get shot? Yes. And you would have fried to a crunchy hunk of a guy!"

He scoffed. "Seriously? If you had listened, I would not be here. Nor you. But you never listen, do you? I speak, and anything I say goes in one lovely ear and out the opposite. I would think it impossible with the marvelous brain lodged in there. Of all the times to *not* listen to me, Lily? This could have ended. We'd both be in our beds for much-needed rest. And as far as the new hole?" He smirked. "I spared you getting it. You are welcome for that too."

Lily blew a raspberry. "If I hadn't found your plan so ludicrous, perhaps I would have gone along with it—" she tilted her head, and a smile curved her lips. "Did you just say I had lovely ears? And a marvelous brain?" She sighed and fidgeted. "I always had a problem listening, Evan. It's not just you. It's everyone." She shrugged. "When you aren't pretty with sisters who are, you have to be loud even to be noticed. Or seen." She did a slight shudder, hugged herself, and checked out their surroundings. "Where are we, anyway?"

"I rarely notice your sisters." But he always noticed Lily. Someone so full of vibrant life made it impossible. Not that he would disclose it to her. Evan reached down to pluck his shirt from the floor, only to find Lily needed to cut it off to reach his wound. Dropping it, he opened a supply cabinet near the tube entrance. "Substation located under the store. I blurred in. Maine occupied the two men with a ruse of a negotiation. I tasked Bailey with hostage removal and rescue." He turned his head to address her and narrowed his gaze. "One that is now a failed rescue. I don't handle failure very well, Lily."

"I..." She uncrossed her arms only to cross them again, lowering her head to stare at the floor with a shrug. "I just can't believe you took the risk. We have hundreds of fighters on the Grid. Why you?" Her eyes alone lifted to regard him. "Do you have any idea how tragic it would have been if you were killed? Bounce barely has a life now. If something happened to you?" She shook her head. "It would be a colossal hit to everyone."

*You too, Lily? Would you find it a loss? A hit?*

Evan mentally erased that line of pondering from going any further. This was not the place. Nor the time. Clearing his throat, he found a tee in the cabinet, shook out the dust from it, and tugged it on. "Thank you for your concern about the hierarchy of command of the Grid."

***

HEARING Evan saying it *that* way, it sounded ridiculous. Lily decided not to compound his impression of her being an idiot and dropped the subject. She tugged the mattress that was on the floor over to the cot and dropped to sit. She had dragged it from its place to lay him on to tend his wounds. There was no chance of her lifting Evan to the cot. All that lean muscle. Not to mention, tall. When she found a large volume of the blood after removing his vest, she feared he had bled out. Doing so would be the reason for him losing consciousness. She had panicked and frantically searched for medical supplies. Finding a med kit with an expiration date three years ago, she tended to Evan's gunshot wound and prayed he didn't develop sepsis and die. Again.

Everyone on the Grid trained for simple field triage, but Lily's mother had been a healer, and her sister Emma was now the lead healer on the Grid. Lily held better knowledge than most.

Her hands had trembled as she stitched him up, whispering to him not to die. She had watched his chest rise and fall with each breath, willing him to do it again and for his ribcage to expand and contract.

As she worked on Evan's wound, her mind recalled how solid and strong he felt under her palms. Lean, rippled muscles with a dusting of light brown hair, and though she would admit it to no one, even if her life counted on it, she found her focus travel from his wound, down a honey trail of fine hair, over his six-pack abs and belly button. She wondered if what rested below his jeans was as impressive as the rest of the man. *He is unconscious, girl. Shake it off.*

Most of the women and some men had fantasies of Evan; his brooding nature teamed with his movie-star handsome looks. Sure, she found him good looking—a fiercer version of the celebrity Ryan Reynolds without the adorable sense of humor. Lily doubted Evan had one at all. She couldn't recall a single time she had heard him tell a joke. Laugh with humor rather than sarcasm. She found it either sad or irritating. Lily wasn't sure which. Maybe both, if possible.

Wait. Did he say he hadn't slept or eaten? Why was that? Sure, Evan was obsessively dedicated. He didn't know the shop customers or Desi, and he must know Beth could take care of herself. The Grid had human trained soldiers without the sun issue—Evan had the power to designate any one of them to do the rescue. Did she dare think it was because of *her?*

"Shit." Evan barked the single curse word. It forced Lily out of her thoughts.

"What is it?"

"Does your stamp work?" He stood tensely at one of the monitor stations and appeared more stressed than usual.

"What? Oh, it didn't work when we first got in here. I tried." She rose to her feet and touched it again. "It's still not working." She looked up sharply in alarm. "Evan! Why aren't our stamps working?"

"I don't know." She asked again, and he repeated by yelling. "I *don't* know!"

Lily squeezed her eyes shut to stop panic from overwhelming her. She was trembling as it began to rise. Lily received her stamp in childhood. Earlier than most people. But then again, other children didn't have both parents murdered in front of them. She grew used to its constant slight electronic humming under the surface of the dark mark on her skin. While other children carried a security blanket to soothe, the stamp did the same for her. Knowing it provided contact with headquarters, she could be rescued, saved, or found easily as others did with a cell phone. It made her feel safe. It assisted in forming the framework for the facade of confidence covering the insecurity beneath. Without the assistance it provided, insecurity would bubble up. She would drown in waves of vulnerability and shame.

"Lily, listen to me."

She opened her eyes to find Evan stood there. His arms rested on her shoulders. Lily focused on his deep hazel eyes, pulled off a nod, but still trembled. Her tone shook. No way to hide her treading the emotional water. "I am."

When Lily went pale and trembled, Evan thought perhaps his earlier scrutiny missed an unseen injury. When she opened her eyes and met his, he saw fear. An overwhelming sense of it fed the tremble. Her voice, usually too loud and bold, sounded small and scared like a little girl. Evan knew he needed to tread lightly to bring her to the reality of their situation.

"A shot hit the communication equipment. Normally, that would not be an issue, having since developed our stamps technology. However"—his gaze slid upward to the ceiling about them—"I think the machine used to enter here is still in an open position. Therefore, security measures registered this substation as compromised. It engaged a jamming system between here and the outside."

Her eyes went wide, and her mouth opened. Fuck, the trembling began again under his palms.

"What are you saying, Evan?" She jerked away from him. "No. There's got to be a way for us to let them know we're in here! To tell them we're safe!" She rushed over to the blur pad and pointed. "This is how you got in here, right? Then let's get out of here! Evan!"

Evan had seen an uncountable number of people lose their shit in battle. Grown men sob like children in fields of blood, praying to any ancient and modern god or goddess when the tides turned toward a defeat, fighters trained to confront enemies and face death as easily as humans went to mundane jobs.

But Lily was no fighter. And while she and her sisters faced the war braver than most noncombat personnel, warriors they were never hardened to be. The one thing he admired most about the three sisters—they were able to be themselves despite the pressure of their world. Lily's current manic state revealed to him the pressure did get to her and was cracking her quick.

"Lily, stop." He reached, took her hand in his, and tugged her back to him. "When it's jammed and locked down, no in or out not only applies to the ability to communicate but impacts our ability to leave. I need you to calm down." He searched her eyes for calm and found none for her to grasp. He'd have to provide it. "You aren't here alone. I'm here with you. We're in this together. But I need you to breathe. Can you do that with me?" He reached out to place his palm on her chest. "In. And out. Slowly with me."

Her gaze darted around the bunker, but at his touch, it locked to his. He felt her breathing slow slightly but still a quick, fluttered pace. He remained concerned. Taking the hand he held, he spread fingers over his chest for her to mimic. "Slowly. Feel mine. In. And out."

Her body shuddered, her breathing slowed, and within a few beats, her heart rate synced up with the rhythm of his. He rewarded her with a smile. "There you go. Good job. Now close your eyes and focus solely on your breathing." He began to move his hand from her, but she reached up to keep it in place. She pressed her palm firmer against his chest. Fine, if it comforted her. He had no problem with it. Her skin was delectably warm through his shirt. His palm nestled between her breasts—not a bad place to be. Not at all. His thumb itched to stroke the spot, but he resisted. The slope of her breast deliciously yet innocently performed the task for him with each rise of her chest.

"Okay. Uh, Evan?"

He stared at her chest without conscious thought of doing so. And judging by how she said his name, Lily was aware he did. Sliding his gaze to hers, he found her eyes wide open with a brow raised. Evan jerked his palm from her and took a step back to sever their connection. "Good. Your breathing is stable. Right. Good." *Come on, Evan. Are you seriously letting touching her tit make your brain incapable of functioning? Snap out of it, moron.*

LILY SMIRKED in amusement at Evan's failed attempt to hide checking out her boobs. However, the humor from Evan showing a normal male behavior assisted with easing the panic. For that, she was grateful. "What now? What do we do?"

Evan rubbed a hand over his face. She could tell he was analyzing their possible next steps. Lily gave the man a ton of shit for being so uptight and regimented, but in this situation, no one would be better to resolve it.

"Let me think." Evan stood and turned to the side. His muscles tensed and relaxed. Lily creatively guessed the flexing reflected the current of thoughts in his head. Bulging biceps, strong corded forearms—flex. Relax. Flex again. Thought. Repeat. Lily made a note to find ways for Evan to have reasons to do this mental workout routine more often. An idea of playing Trivial Pursuit with Evan would be a visual treat for a woman. Perhaps stack the deck so he had the hardest question cards to do *a lot* of that thought process. Shirtless.

The gleeful thought of Evan playing board games without a shirt led Lily's wonderment to take in the sight of his ass. Oh, look. He did a full body flex there too. Did naked Trivia Pursuit exist? Lily was game to find out. She'd Google it when they got out of this mess. Oo, nude Jenga? That game might be better than trivia, all that wood involved. Hard. Solid. Wood.

"Lily, are you listening?"

She blinked and nodded her head—a little too fast. "Oh, no. I wasn't. But I am now." Sheesh. Blowing out a breath, she shook her hands to ease her nerves. He narrowed his eyes but didn't ask what occupied her thoughts. *Whew...*

"We need to move that cooler above. That may, I hope, remove the substation from its locked-down state. I can then blur us both out."

He moved past her to go to the tunnel, and Lily reached out to stop him. "Wait. No. They could be waiting. In fact, they most likely are. And what happens if you get gunned down?" *What happens to me? What would they do to me?* She swallowed, dropped her hands, and then wrapped her arms around herself. "I..." She brought her eyes to his. "And it's daytime. How do you know the sun hasn't reached this end of the store? It was close before we came down here."

Evan's handsome brow creased, and his jaw flexed as he considered. "No one knows we are down here. As far as the others are concerned, we are still being held hostage above. The longer we wait, the harder that will be on them. The more drastic measures they'll take."

Lily's eyes trailed up the tube. She knew he was most likely correct. The thought he'd be shot or even killed, freaked her the F out. She heard dull thuds above their heads—footfalls on the door. Charlie and Kyle must be trying to figure out a way to get in. *Good luck, boys. The Grid doesn't mess around when it comes to security.*

"I know. But whatever actions they take, we're safe down here, right? And if they bomb the place or snipers shoot it full of holes, we're still safe." Evan's determined expression led Lily to believe her logic held little sway on what plans he would concoct. "Let's just give it a little more time. At least until we know the sun has set. Maybe those two will realize they can't get to us and give up."

Evan opened his mouth to counter before he then paced away. "Excellent point. Once they take them down or those two surrender, the first place the Grid will check is here. To ensure it wasn't compromised."

The relief flooding through Lily when he agreed made her knees weaken. "I need to sit down." Exhaling slowly, she sank to the cot. "I actually can't believe you agreed with me. On that. On anything."

She ran her hands nervously through her hair and reached up to secure it in a ponytail. The stuff was so damn thick and unruly as always. It never cooperated, but an attempt was better than the tangled mess now. "We just need to wait. Right?" She nibbled on her bottom lip. "How long could it take? Those guys don't want to be here. No way. And Bounce and the rest will want to end this." She closed her eyes. "This will be over in no time."

"*Y*ou should eat."

Lily sat in silence while Evan attempted to get the communication equipment working on any functioning level. Touching together wires to use Morse code would have thrilled him. He'd possibly do a little happy dance. But it was as dead as he had once been. Finding the newest of the aged MREs and two bottled water, he sat to lean against the wall in front of her. "Lily, here."

"I'm claustrophobic." She took the package of food and water. "I like to think I have a great handle on it until something like this"—she motioned to the surrounding space—"happens, and that handle is nowhere to be found."

Evan's eyes were downcast, examining the food within the wrapped MRE. Peanut butter, dried cranberries, and sticks of what appeared to be jerky. As Lily spoke, he listened with a grunt, acknowledging he was paying attention to her statements. He chewed and shrugged as she fell into silence. "Many have that same affliction. It's nothing to be ashamed of."

"But it is, for me." She rose with the supplies untouched on the cot next to her and paced. "It all started when my parents were killed. In that van."

Evan's eyes tracked her movements but remained quiet—unsure if this was a two-way conversation or she needed to vent solo.

"Our parents told us to stay in the van. They locked the doors when the ambush happened. I sat there. Watched them be massacred." She laughed the saddest sound Evan had ever heard. "And I kept thinking I wouldn't be able to go school shopping the next day." She let out a pained sob. "My parents were getting killed, and I thought that. I was trapped in that van. Maybe my mind didn't want to comprehend what had taken place right in front of me. And when it did," she whispered as her hands came up to cover her face, "I felt the van squeezing in on me. The walls growing thinner. Less air. I felt as if I were suffocating with each slam of the demons against the van. The weaker I thought the metal became, the easier for the killers to reach me. To kill me. My sisters and brother. I became hysterical to escape, which was stupid. The killers were *outside*. I fought to get out. And Emma, Rose, and Ben screamed for me to stop. But all I could do was scream over and over, 'Let me out.'" She slid down the wall to sit across from him. "Every time I'm in a space like that, like this, I have to shut it down, you know? Disconnect that here is not there, then." She sighed. "That sounded pathetic. Jesus, I'm pitiful."

Evan reached over to pluck the supplies off the cot and slid them over to her. "We all have fears, Lily. And we find ourselves in situations causing them to surface."

Lily laughed bitterly as she ripped open the package and picked at it. Evan specifically gave her the MRE containing trail mix and chocolate. With some sort of dried fruit. He knew she enjoyed chocolate. Most females did. He noticed at Grid functions she always picked the chocolate treats placed for attendees. He may have watched her eat them in complete enjoyment—both her devouring and him discreetly viewing her pleasure.

"You have fears, Evan? I find that hard to believe. If you do, you're damn good at hiding them."

Evan snorted and blew out a slow exhale. "I'll give you that one." He angled his head to regard her. "I didn't know you were claustrophobic. But this place isn't too bad. I've lived in homes smaller, shittier, and much worse." He frowned and rubbed the back of his neck. He did not intentionally wish to go anywhere close to the subject his comparison dug up.

With Evan's mood shift, Lily reached out to touch his knee. "Evan, where'd you go?"

He looked down at it and then lifted his eyes to hers with a frown. "The past. And fears." He swallowed and sat back. "I lived in a one-room flat once. Smaller than this. And not as nice, if you can imagine."

Her hand remained in place as she asked softly, "I don't think I've ever heard about your past. Your human life."

Evan raised a brow. "I have found no reason to discuss it. The past is just that. But regarding fears, mine is repeating it."

Lily's features creased with puzzled concern. She moved to sit next to him. "Evan, the past can only happen once. Contrary to history. It can repeat, sure. There are volumes of history books written about that very thing for us to learn from. But our past? It's done. The day ends, and the next begins. Done. No need to fear it."

Evan cranked his head sharply to the side to glare at her with a sneer. "It must be easy to say that when you haven't existed an immortal century with guilt and shame. And the loss—"

Loud bangs interrupted him. He jerked Lily up to her feet as he stood. Placing her behind him, he slid his gun belt from the counter. "They're trying to breach." Releasing his 9mms from the holsters, he walked stiffly to stand under the tunnel entrance, aiming his guns above in preparation to fire if the robbers somehow broke through. The percussions of what he assumed were bullets struck the metal. He had high confidence their efforts would fail. However, over the decades, the ancient substation became coated with rust. Earthquakes damaged the structure. Its integrity was questionable, including the only separation between them and the men above.

The sounds ended, and Evan smirked when he heard the two men curse. He was a son of a bitch to hope the two bastards had a quick lesson on velocity and rebound dynamics of a ricocheting bullet. Sadly, no thud of a body. It diminished his glee at the possibility one or both of the men had been killed. Their foolish demise would have made things so much easier.

Turning, he found Lily standing with legs apart and arms braced to attack with a water bottle in her hands. Completely adorable. It defused Evan's defensive mode instantly. "What would you do with that, exactly?"

Lily's gaze jerked to the water bottle she held in her hand. "It's all I had. Or could find. It's better than nothing."

Evan couldn't help the laugh following her declaration. "You are something else."

However, the bottle flying toward his head informed Evan she found nothing funny.

"Of course you're laughing at me. Go ahead. Men like you always do."

Evan's humor vanished at the tone of her words. "Men like me?" He holstered his guns and cocked his head to the side. "Really? I'd love to be educated." He waved his palm in her direction as he sat on the counter. "Continue. Please."

Lily snorted and looked upward as she crossed her arms. "Yeah, like you. Good looking, smug, think you are all that." She stepped up to him and got within inches of his face. "Guys like you that can have any woman they want. And have. And *never* give me *any* notice or consideration. Like, I'm the ugly fruit in the sex market." Her shoulders came up, and she laughed—a bitterly cold sound. "My sisters, sure. Beautiful. Thin. Badasses. But because I wore glasses and was chubby, I spent my time in books about history. I'm what?" She stepped back and laughed again. "Not as worthy of being desired? Less valuable? Never taken seriously? God, it gets so old!"

Evan narrowed his eyes and leaned back against the wall. "And you are lumping me with men who—" but she continued without a pause as if she hadn't heard him. More likely, she had once again refused to listen. Evan was unsure she had even bothered to take a breath between sentences. Eyes fiery, her posture far was more threatening in her indignant rant than earlier when she was ready to fight with a bottle of water. Fiercely beautiful.

"I know—boy, do I know—I'm no size five. Or even a size *ten*, but I am smart. I have a sharp mind. I am a wonderful person who cares! And I have a heart, just like any other woman. But over and over, I get discounted because of the way I look, how I don't fit the mold of what men want! So why even try. Either a guy accepts me as I am, or he can go to hell." She pointed her finger at him, and Evan noticed tears shimmered on her long lashes. "That includes you, Evan O'Brien!"

## 11

"*A*re you done? Get it all out of your system?" Evan moved from the wall and walked toward her. There wasn't anywhere Lily could go. He caged her in with his arms when her back found the wall. His hands moved to press on either side of her head as he leaned in to lock eyes. "You are wrong. Wrong about me. And most definitely, undeniably incorrect about yourself."

Swallowing, Lily met his intensity head-on. "I don't need one of your pep talks, E. I know what kind of girl you go for. You have a reputation as a ladies' man. The one-night stand mentality that all of you alpha males on the Grid have. You like them with big tits, fake eyelashes, and painted Botox plumped red lips. Bedroom eyes and they ask no questions. Brains that aren't equal to the task or don't care any more than you do to ask or want more." She bowed toward him and came as close as she could without touching. "And in case you didn't know? I'm a woman. Not a girl. And I don't slut myself out or want less than I deserve." She shoved her hand against his chest to back him off. "Which is everything. So I will be happy to have *nothing* if I can't get it." She lifted her chin. "And I never beg. I haven't since I was a little girl stuck in a van."

Evan's eyes took on a hooded look, the hazel color darkening, and his fangs showing as he spoke. "You think you have me figured out, Lily? That you know my type?"

He was too close. Lily felt fear creeping up. She could smell him—the manly scent of sweat mixed with gunpowder, a heady scent, more teasing than the most expensive cologne. A day's growth of whiskers shaded his jaw, hair unkempt. The wild combination made him more feral, more attractive—pure man caging the soul of a hungry beast.

Lily's gaze slid along his strong jawline and halted on his bared fangs. Why had she never dared to think Evan restrained a wild side? Others waved theirs as a fuck flag to the opposite sex. All the fighters on the Grid carried sexual boldness unabashedly for all to see—strutting like deadly peacocks and peahens with arrogant confidence. But not Evan. Always steady, reliable, unwavering, controlled Evan.

Until now. Did she do that? Impossible. Lily refused to believe she was capable of having that effect on any man, much less Evan O'Brien. And if so, she should stop pushing him to see how intense this could go. Shouldn't she?

Of course not.

"I know I'm *not* your type. I'm no man's type, Evan. It's that easy." She once again tried to escape, but his arms wouldn't give, that broad muscled chest like a wall under her palm. "Move."

He smiled, and the way it curved his lips reminded Lily of a cat with a mouse pinned under its paw, deciding to play with its prey or eat it. Evan would find that a trapped Lily did not give up without a fight.

"Let me enlighten you, Ms. Devenmore, exactly what type of woman I do like." He moved his hand. Rather than give her an opening to escape, he wrapped his fingers around a lock of her hair. "I like my women strong. An easy conquest is dull. Blondes are boring to me. Redheads are overhyped—believe it. Brunettes? Impossible to typeset into any one description." His eyes followed the motion as he ran the back of his knuckles across her jaw. His thumb traced her bottom lip. "I like my females like these lips. Full and lush. And speaking of fruit, my favorite is a ripe, warm peach. Fresh and heated from the sun. Waiting, almost beckoning me to take a bite. It may be bitter. It may be sweet"—his head came down to whisper, breath tickling her ear—"but you'll devour it nonetheless because you hungrily craved that fucking peach."

His eyes remained with hers. Lily refused to play the game of visual chicken. His hand warm on her skin, his words, the way he stated them, created a warm puddle of need inside of her. God, she wanted to be that peach—until he spat it out—not to his liking. Too rough and soured. Not equal to the craving. He'd pick another peach, and she'd be the pit left behind. No. She was smarter than that. History did indeed repeat itself.

"I'm no peach, Evan." She hissed through her teeth, tempted to lick his thumb where it remained on her lip. She jerked from his touch. "Peaches don't bite back."

"No. You are a unique type of fruit, one with hardened skin. Protecting the tender, sweet essence beneath it. Afraid of being bitten and then tossed." His gaze broke their battle, but where they went had Lily feeling hotter. Evan's scrutiny spiked her temperature, blazing a path from her face to below, over her nipples growing taut, and liquid heat between her legs. He grazed her jawline with his fingers and then boldly stroked the curves of her breast at the neckline of her tee. "You are so fucking beautiful. Every time you pissed me off, aggravated the shit out of me, I always let you walk away first. And it had nothing to do with my command or duty, Lily. It had to do with lusting for you to walk away. So I could watch those hips. Those long, thick legs carry you off and your ass... It, too, reminds me of a peach." His eyes angled back to hers. "I wanted to bite it." One corner of his lips slipped up. "Still do."

"I would have kicked you in the balls," she responded in a gasp. Her hitched breath gave her away—made it hard to breathe.

Too close. And zero to do with claustrophobia. Evan penetrated the air, wove into her lungs. Sought out her soul.

Evan brought his lips to her ear. His arm snaked around her waist to pull her closer, molding their bodies together. Just him, her, and a wall. With no place to go. "Are you sure *that's* what you want to do with my balls, Lily?"

She sucked in a breath and squeezed her eyes shut. This situation was unadulterated insanity. Locked in a dusty, crappy bunker. She hadn't had a shower in over twenty-four hours now, and Evan—"Mr. Stick-in-the-Ass"—was the very last man she should entertain a toss on the cot with.

Struggling to revive her shielded facade, she smiled. "Fuck you, Evan."

"For once, Lily, we agree."

Before Lily could ask him to elaborate, his mouth captured hers in a blistering kiss. Borderline cruel and unrelenting in demand, but she spurred him to increase it. One hand twisted his shirt. The other went up to fist his hair. Nothing remained between them other than clothes as Evan's hard, lean body pressed into her curves seductively. So very, very wicked.

Gasping for air, she dragged her mouth from his and sagged against the wall. His mouth nipped along her jaw as it traveled to her neck. Oh god, fangs... Most women would never know the pure eroticism of a lover with fangs. *Not your lover. And he won't want to be—stop this. You need to...*

He bit her.

*Hello, turn on. Goodbye, brain.*

She let out a moan as she felt the clamp of Evan's teeth on her skin. Not enough to break the flesh but enough to claim her. If only for a little while. Warm palms, roughened by gun and blade hilts, slid under her shirt to free her breasts.

He whispered lustfully, "I've thought of these so many times, Lily."

Those words, for whatever reason, acted as icy water on Lily's feverish arousal. "Wait, wait!"

Evan took two steps back to put his arms out to the side. "What is it? Lily, I want you. I've wanted you for years."

Lily shook her head. "You thought about it. About me. Imagined what I looked like without clothes, right?"

"So many times. You have no idea. And I'd be ashamed to tell you the amount," Evan replied with a throaty chuckle. "If I did, I'm pretty sure you'd throw it back in my face until the end of time."

He stepped forward to return, and she put a palm between them to stop him. "Then take my word for it that my body is not the things of fantasies." She looked to the side and brought a hand up to wipe her eyes. "I can't even look at myself nude in the mirror. If you think I'm anything like my sisters, I'm not. I guess they took after my mother. I, unfortunately, took after my father." She let out a ragged sigh and faced him. "I'm not beautiful. That's very sweet for you to say, Evan, but we both know you can't do your job if you're blind." She looked away from him. The look of raw need would crumble her resolve, and she wouldn't ruin his fantasies with her reality. "How about we try to think about how bad of an idea this is." She blushed at the way he continued to look at her as if her reasoning held no impact. She flushed at the thought of him seeing more of her. Part of her wanted that. Most of her dreaded it. "That way, you don't have to see me naked."

WOULD LILY EVER CEASE to baffle and aggravate him? Most likely not. But over time, it added a spicy flavor to his attraction to her. He'd have to give it to the Devenmore sisters, the three of them were a delightful challenge. "You're wrong. I never once looked at your sisters and thought about taking them to bed. About how they looked without clothes. Not a single time. But you." He approached her boldly, closing the space between them. He had to feel those soft curves against him again. To be in her space and breathe in the salty, spiced scent of her skin. "I wanted to taste that mouth. Claim those lips. Make you scream in a different way." He smiled, and it must have reflected the sinful thoughts running in his mind judging by the widening of Lily's eyes. Her mouth formed an *O* with a gasp.

He traveled his attention slowly down her body from head to toes and dipped his head to hover his mouth right above hers. "I can't fuck you if we keep our clothes on, Lily." One hand came up next to her head to brace them against the wall, and then the other joined it. "And we will fuck. Perhaps we'll do it twice. And you will enjoy it. And trust me, so will I."

Then he kissed her as she sucked in a breath, and judging by her hands clutching at his clothes in need, twice became an actual possibility. Evan was a fan of math.

12

*S*tall. Lily needed to stall. Anything to allow this erotic game of cat and mouse that she and Evan were engaged in to continue but without going into his trap entirely. No way did she wish it to end. But when she had to undress with his eyes on her, he'd put on the brakes. When Evan O'Brien, the man Lily was a few corners short of peeking around and becoming a stalker, would see her naked, it would awkwardly stop.

What if he laughed? Or worse—gave her a look of disgust? It would crumble her ego. Slaughter what fragile self-confidence she had slowly attempted to weave. What if he was a kiss-and-tell kind of guy? She found that hard to believe, but she also thought him ever wanting to have sex with her equally unbelievable.

His hands swept under her shirt, and he moaned with pleasure as he cupped her breasts, kneading and teasing. And he had an erection. She felt it hard and thick against her thigh as their hips ground together. She wondered what it felt like in her hand, tasted like in her mouth. Flicking her tongue over the head and tasting prec—

*God! Stop it. Do not go down that path. Stop thinking about his cock! Get it together, Lily.* But wait—going down would be a great way to delay the inevitable. And if she got him off? She might avoid the naked reveal altogether.

Forcing her mouth away from his, she gulped for air and went to her knees in front of him. She worked his belt buckle, then his jeans button-fly, and reached inside to free him. And boy howdy, did she have her hands full. Lifting her eyes to his, she smiled at him. "You know, we had a betting pool once on how big all the Breakers were. You had pretty good odds."

Evan smirked and gave a lusty laugh. "Really? Who won?"

"Sure you want to know?" Lily winced playfully. "Jess. Sorry. If it helps, you were in the top five."

Before he could retort, she wrapped her mouth around the tip of his cock and then took him in. One delicious, inch by inch... Her wondering about his taste was satisfied as she worked down his shaft until she reached the soft brown hair at the base. He tasted all male. Salty yet somehow delicious. Like sprinkling salt on ice cream. If it was hot. And pulsing. And ice cream was able to grow thicker and longer with each lick instead of melting. Lily was the one melting into a puddle of need.

Evan's hands came down to twist her hair away from her face. Lily knew men liked to watch the action, and Evan was no exception. If there was one sexual act that Lily had perfected since high school, it was performing a blow job. Every guy liked it. Some guys only wanted it. And just as in this situation, Lily stayed dressed doing it. Cookies, hah. Let her sisters have that. Oral sex was Lily's superpower.

Using her hand to tease and stroke, her tongue curled and lips sucked, Evan moaned and jacked his hips to orchestrate her motion. Flicking her eyes up, she lost her rhythm for a moment at the view above her. Evan's face was tense. His eyes were closed and mouth open. Veins stood out on his neck, pulsated on his arms. The same muscles flexed earlier were in full glory times ten during sex. The sight of him in passion would make her orgasm without a single strip of clothes lost. Evan looked glorious during sex. Even this juvenile form of it.

Her slowing of motion caught his attention, desire blazing in those brown eyes when they drifted down to find hers. He had popped free of her mouth, springing out to tap her in the face in a fleshy "hello, remember me" gesture. He chuckled, and she blushed.

"Get lost? Forget what we were doing?" His voice was hoarse with desire and a hint of an Irish accent. It was sweet but also sad. Evan could only truly relax during sex. No wonder he used it often as an escape.

Lily licked her lips and gave a shy smile. "No. Not lost. Just sightseeing." She curled her hand back around his cock and leaned in to continue. Before she got her lips wrapped around him, his hands came down under her arms to lift her to her feet. She mewled at the loss—he wasn't the only one enjoying the oral play.

"Since you wandered off the path, let's get to the destination." His mouth went to her neck, and there were those fangs again. Good lord, did all beings with fangs have the superpower of making a girl's brain stop working? No wonder some women and men at Bounce's club became fang-bangers.

"Evan, wait." She gasped as his hands wandered. One cupped her breast and the other over her ass. "Please. Wait…"

Evan's hands stilled. "Lily, are we going to do this again?" He shifted back enough to look at her, amusement evident in his expression, mixed with the desire. "I believe your mouth found evidence of how much I want you." His hand came down to curl around hers, still wrapped on his shaft. Oops, Lily had forgotten it was still there. "And I continue to want you. Actually, it's getting harder at the thought of having you. Mouth no longer there or not." He searched her eyes a little more intensely than Lily wished. She turned her head to the side in desperate hopes of not giving into him. No chance of it, she knew. But can't blame a girl for trying.

"What if I disappoint you?" she asked in a whisper. Partly out of embarrassment. A little out of fear. Hard-on aside, did he genuinely want to be with her? His hands must have felt how soft she was. No flat tummy here. Well, his rippled with a six-pack stomach didn't count.

Evan sighed as he lifted her chin. "Lily, you have not once disappointed me. Challenged me? Definitely. Pissed me off? Without a doubt." He brushed his lips over hers. "Been fuckable? Always." His eyes were back to probing hers. "Don't be scared. I only want to make this good for both of us. Trust me."

*Hah, trust him.* How could she trust any man? Time and time again, she had tried romance. Some men ghosted her after the first date. Others took her to bed only to be gone the next morning. She made them turn the lights off every time. The two relationships going further had ended in heartache. One due to a quick marriage followed by an even faster divorce straight out of high school. The other... well, not the right place or time to go into the details of that. And definitely not with Evan.

Lily let out a shaky laugh. "You say that, but I'm not the one who fantasized about me." That was a fib—she had spent time with her buzzy friend to the thought of Evan and her. She had witnessed him working out in only shorts. Watched the man do chin-ups like a creep around the corner. No shame. Zero. None. She even attempted to do it again. Sadly, the opportunity didn't present itself a second time. Not for the lack of Lily trying.

"I want you. But more than that, I want you to believe me when I say it." He stepped back and pulled his shirt off to toss to the side. Next, he slid his jeans down and kicked them free. Toeing off his boots and socks, he stood there. A lot of him "stood" there. Muscles. More muscles, and how in any anatomical way did he have a larger erection than before? *Daammmmnn.*

Lily's throat went dry, her mouth fell open, and she sputtered. "Wow. You're just, wow."

Evan smirked. "I'm no cowboy."

A nervous giggle bubbled up and triggered a full laugh.

The laugh did not thrill Evan. In fact, he scowled. And it made Lily laugh harder. "Oh, no, no. I'm not laughing at the two of you." Her hand motioned to the man and his penis. "You are... beautiful. I've never seen a man so beautiful." She swallowed and could still taste him. "Evan..."

"Stop. Stop thinking. Stop doubting." He cupped her face in his hands and captured her mouth in a kiss. Angling his head to dip his tongue in, she let out a moan of pleasure. Beautifully built from head to toe and could kiss better than any other man she had ever kissed.

His hands gripped the hem of her shirt and began to lift. She grasped his wrist to stop him, but when his eyes came to hers, all she found was heat.

Burning. Sizzling. Wanton. Unabashed heat. For her.

Exhaling slowly, the shirt was lifted over her head and thrown to the floor. Evan's hand came up to cup one breast as the other slid around her to unclasp her bra. It joined the heap of clothes at their feet. Lily brought her hands up to cover her face. She could smell the male scent of his most masculine part on her palms. Erotic. Like sex in cologne form.

"Lily, I'd like to see your face. You got to see mine. It's only fair that I see yours."

His syllables rolled with more of that sexy Irish accent. Apparently, the more aroused, the more his true self emerged. The more heated, the more Irish. Delicious as the rest of him. Letting out a breath to steady herself, Lily dropped her hand but kept her eyes closed.

She felt his hands on her waist. Then the snap of her jeans followed by the zipper as it loosened. Cool air touched her thighs as he slid them down. Evan let out a low growl, and it sent thrilling goose bumps from Lily's head to her toes. Still wearing her boy short panties, the chill on her skin transitioned to a heated brush of air. The source of it became clear as Evan's mouth touched her through the silk of cloth. Wet and teasing. Lily groaned as she fisted his hair, nails digging into his scalp. Oh, he was good. Apparently, Lily wasn't the only one with oral sex superpowers.

Her body sagged back, bowed over him with the wall once again at her back. Both her hands pinned his head in place. She was afraid he'd stop, and oh god, the last thing she wanted was a halt. Cool air once again touched her. This time in the most heated part of her, only for it to be replaced by Evan's mouth as he slid the panties off. Lily's head came down, eyes came open, and she watched Evan work her folds and nip with those fangs. No way could she hold back her climax with the sensations and the sight of him. She slapped a hand over her mouth to stifle the scream as she shook with the intensity of it.

Evan moved up her body, kissing his way up. Her eyes fluttered open in a sensual haze and found him smiling. "You taste amazing. Fantasy is on point so far."

Lily's ragged breathing made it difficult to speak. She endeavored to try. "That's. Good. To know." Evan was shrewd. He used her blitzed condition to step back. His focus ran over her with such animalistic need that she found it impossible to move to hide from it. Like prey hoping if it stayed still, the predator would not find its next meal in her. Move on for a more tempting focus of the hunt.

"Did you know that the Greeks and other artisans carved goddesses with the same curves, dips, and valleys you possess, Lily baby?" Her breath caught as he grazed the back of his hand from her breasts to her hip and gripped. Pulling her against him, he let out another of those yummy snarls. "I like my women full. I can grab, and they can take it as I dive in. More skin to lick, bite, and command. I don't want the type of woman you misbelieved I did."

His head dipped down to bite her neck, this time piercing the skin. Oh, fucking Jesus. It should have hurt. She felt her hot blood drip before his tongue lapped at the flow. He suckled her, and her knees went weak. She knew he would catch her without a wiggle in the faith.

One position Lily always found as her number one would be held aloft, legs wrapped around a lover's waist, and taken against the wall. Rough and hard. One problem with the desire—fear the man would figure out her weight. Then they would struggle to perform because of it. As with being nude in front of a man, she found a way to avoid it. But none of them were Evan O'Brien. Strong and solid. She even bought believing he lusted for more of her. She'd trust it for now. He gave her no reason not to.

Lily brought one leg up to curve around his flexing ass as he ground into her as he fed. She hoped he'd take the hint for what she wanted. He wasn't the only one who fantasized about having sex together.

He took her cue as if a mind reader. For all Lily knew, he possessed that gift. If so, she'd shield her thoughts later. But not in this. It was an aspect that worked to her advantage.

When he pulled his fangs free with a snarl, his hands moved to her thighs and lifted her as if she weighed nothing. Lily's hair fell over her face, and he effortlessly kept her against the wall with one arm, as the other hand gently swept the locks back.

Both of them panted, and Lily felt his hardness against her core. Parking her forehead on his, she gave him a wicked smile. "Well, if I'm a goddess, you better get to worshiping, O'Brien."

13

*e died because of you. Are you going to get her killed too, Evan? With your job. With your sense of duty. Even if it's wrong and costs you everything?"*

*The volume of the child's crying changed decibel with each pause between the sentences. A low wailing during the pause between each word. Painfully loud. Evan squeezed his eyes closed tightly to avoid looking at her. Her and the toddler were decimated and thin, skin pale and yellowed with disease.*

Evan screamed pleas for forgiveness.

"Evan, it's okay. It was a nightmare. It's not real. Wake up!"

Disoriented, he searched frantically in the dim light to find Lily's face. She hovered above him, and for a heartbeat, he thought somehow she too was trapped inside of his night terror. But no, they remained in the bunker. He pulled away and scrubbed his hands over his eyes. "Fuck," he grumbled. That detailed brand nightmare of his past hadn't visited Evan in years. What a dumbass to believe his mind had lost the details to construct it. Maybe the situation spawned it, but whatever the trigger, he didn't want it to become a regular occurrence. For decades, it had.

"Who was she?"

He and Lily lay on the floor. At what point they had landed there, Evan had no idea. Uncomfortably hard, covered in dust, and he felt something painfully jabbing him in the back. However, he wouldn't move whatever it was intruding to puncture a vital organ. Lily was in his arms, head on his chest, and long, silky brown hair teasing his skin. One hand cupped the back of her head, and the other splayed on that delectable ass of hers.

One he bit not just once, but twice, once on each cheek.

Lily liked it. So much, she asked for the second. Being the gentleman that he prided himself to be, he happily granted her request.

"Who was who?" Evan inquired hoarsely. His hand flailed to the side and found a scattered bottle of water. Taking Lily against the wall had caused the supplies to fall from the shelf that was destroyed during his ferocious desire to take her.

"You yelled a name in the nightmare. Liza? Or maybe Lisa? You sounded so tortured. Difficult to tell which." She gently touched his arm. "I'm going to guess a woman who broke your heart. Is she why you haven't had any meaningful relationships since your death?" She looked away as she gathered her hair from her face. "I know you never dated. I do know you—" She stopped herself with a huff. "Well, you had relations. Um… sex. Just not the ship part of the involvement. With others and"—she gathered the blanket to cover herself—"now me. Recently." She brought her eyes to his, and a blush pinkened her cheeks. "Who was she?"

He angled his head to mull the life summary she knew of and frowned. Did he dare open up? Reveal the most intimate parts of his former mortal life he fought to hide? Time built thick walls around it, making it more secure—isolating the sounds, sights, and acrid taste of it, preventing his past from intruding on his present.

Evan cleared his throat, rose to his feet to find his jeans, and slid them on. Fastening them, he stepped over their discarded clothes and beyond Lily's touch. She had crumbled enough of his battlements already. "Um." He raked his fingers through his hair and held the bottle of water to her, then cracked a second open for himself. Draining it, he took in a steadying breath and blew it out slowly. "My wife."

Lily took the water, sat up, and tied the blanket around her. "You had a wife?" Her beautiful features lined in bafflement. Neither she nor others knew about Evan's wife—Bounce became aware at Evan's transition. His boss was shown a flash of any person chosen. Bounce alone had the power to accept or reject those for redemption. He didn't know the painful details. One, the man never asked. And two, it spared Evan from discussing. The weight of it lessened over time and became easier to carry.

Right up to the moment when Lily had asked her question— who was she...

With those three words, his past crashed down with the force of tons, crushing to burst beyond the willpower to contain it. Or maybe just fucking tired of doing so.

"Her name was Liza. Not Lisa. Short for Elizabeth. We met as children, fell in love as teens, and married the first chance we could." He sat on the cot, kept his head down, and fixated on the bottle of water held in his hands. "Both of our parents were Irish immigrants. That shithole I brought up earlier, the same tenement building. A place never made to cram dozens of families into. My parents had one room, others the same—a shared bathroom, and no kitchens. We made meals as we could. Cooked over fires in the litter-filled," air quotes, "*courtyard.*"

"When was this?"

He rubbed his forehead. "I was born in 1897 in Chicago. Uh, I can't tell you the age I met Liza. She was just always a part of my life. When we turned seventeen, we married—a simple exchange of vows, a pitiful wedding celebration consisting of day-old bread and watery soup. We moved into one of the one-room flats. Same building. A few floors up from our parents." He dropped his hand, the empty bottle fisted in his fingers and closed his eyes. "We struggled to scrape together a life worth a damn. People then not only didn't trust immigrants but also didn't want to give them jobs. She went from sweatshop to sweatshop. I attempted to learn a trade. I tried it all. Plumbing. Construction. I did some time as a, well…" He laughed sadly. "Several times, I was a busboy. A cook. Nothing really stuck for me."

He exhaled slowly and stood. He dared not look over at Lily and see her reaction. Perhaps she imagined his a tale of glory and dare. Many persons on the Grid had such backgrounds. Spartans. Gunslingers. Assassins. The life of human Evan O'Brien, not such a glorious tale. Just fucking sad and tragic. Pitiful. He didn't want to see the emotion reflected on Lily's face. Not only would it piss him off, but would shut this storytelling session down.

"We survived that way for years." He let out a bitter laugh. "Funny how time flies, not only when you're having fun but when you can't even find it. We went to bed hungry most nights. Broke without reprieve. Desperate without mercy." Evan's hands pressed over his face, and the heels of his palms ground against his eyes. "Somehow, in the midst of all of that, she got pregnant."

"You had a child?"

Lily asked the question with a soft voice. Gentle. Not pushing him for more of the story. He could quickly stop it right there. Say no more. Her kindness encouraged him to loosen the burden of personal history. His walls fell entirely, and he didn't resist nor wanted to.

"Yes. A little boy named Fredrick. She thought it was a royal sounding name. Not a kid from the slums. We called him Freddy. Such a precocious baby and always happy." He bit the inside of his cheek until he tasted blood, and he looked sideways at the wall. "Even while he starved. Liza couldn't make enough milk, and any other type was impossible to find. Formula did not exist then. Lucky if someone would sell me a quart of goat's milk. We barely had food, and it slowly took its toll. At one point, we scourged up a cup of coarse wheat flour."

He swung his head forward. Lily now stood in front of him with the blanket worn toga-style. He met her eyes, and his voice cracked. "Flour and rust-tainted water do not equal nutrition for a baby. But at least a full belly stopped him from crying." Lily's hand came up to palm his cheek. He pressed closer to her warm touch. "I needed to do something. For her. For Freddy. They'd die in that place, and it would be my fault." He swallowed as emotions choked his voice. "I had to save what mattered to my world. The only thing that did. They made life have value. Without them, what would be the point of having one?."

"Oh my god, E." Tears shimmered in her eyes. Her voice was stilted with sympathy for him. "What did you do?"

His head went back, and his gaze ascended to the low ceiling above. "I essentially bought my ticket to Hell. I became a dangerous man."

14

With each sentence Evan wrenched free, Lily felt her heart rip. It twisted his voice, his face and body tense with anxious nerves. When she lifted her free hand to touch the other cheek, he flinched as if her existence had been forgotten. She hoped that reminding Evan he wasn't alone would bring him back to her. Here and now. "I don't see you ever being a bad man, Evan. You did whatever you had to do to take care of those you loved. I can't imagine how hard that must have been."

He looked away, and she continued to cup his face gently to restore his focus to her. "What happened to them? Liza and Freddy?"

Lily realistically prepared for Evan to shut down. She prayed he wouldn't, but she wouldn't blame him if he did. As far as Lily knew, Evan never showed vulnerability. Surely this wasn't the first time he had allowed himself to be. That wouldn't be a surprise, either—controlled, uptight, hardass Evan. Now Lily knew why he needed to be. Not *wanted*, but needed. She knew all about protective measures, using a coping tactic to avoid dealing with pain. Agony lurked beneath a facade. It held Evan hostage from any future. One with happiness, love…

Her.

And even if it meant he wouldn't find it with her, she wanted Evan to have it with someone.

"What happened, E?"

His eyes locked on hers—flashing deep rage. Lily believed he wasn't directing it at her but toward someone else. "You ever heard of Al Capone? The gangster?"

Lily frowned and lifted a shoulder as she moved to clutch the blanket in her hands. "Of course, I have. I'm a librarian and a history buff. Al Capone. Gang leader, murderer, prohibition, gun runner—" Evan raised a brow. The slight motion cut her off. Realization as the pieces fell together. "You were in the nineteen-twenties. You said you became a dangerous man. Holy shit, Evan. Did you work for Capone?"

He nodded. "Yes. I bused tables at one of his restaurants on the east side. I assume I made some sort of impression. He hired me to collect protection money. Gin transport all over the city. I started out at the bottom and worked my way up. Finally, I was able to support Liza. Give Freddy the life he more than deserved."

He sagged exhausted against the wall. Lily took his hand and led him to the cot. "What year did it start?"

Evan closed his eyes and whispered, "A few months after Freddy was born. I was enlisted by the gang the tail of winter in 1926. By the end of 1928, I stood two men from the top. A driver and enforcer for the right-hand man to Capone. A man by the name of Jack McGurn. We called him Machine Gun after his weapon of choice. But Lily, let's make no mistake. Working for Capone had nothing to do with being evil. A wrong choice was taken." He turned his head to regard her. "I didn't tell Liza. I decided *not* to tell her what my new job entailed. Who I worked for." He closed his eyes. "And in a single moment, I was denied the chance."

<hr>

CHICAGO, FEBRUARY 12TH, 1929

"Liza, I'm home." Evan removed his suit jacket, then his fedora, and hung both on the rack by the door. Turning, he took a moment to appreciate their new place. Clean and newly constructed. The walls still held hints of sawdust. Wide windows pouring in sunlight caused the polished hardwood floors to softly sparkle. Al used his connections to assist Evan to lease it. He and Liza were the only Irish in the place. The price of the rent was steep, but Evan could easily afford it thanks to his boss.

He heard Freddy babble a greeting for his daddy from the corner, and Evan joined him, picking him up into a hug. "Hello, little man. Did you and Mama have a wonderful day?" His son cuddled up against him, and the chatter continued. He tucked Freddy's head under his chin, soft baby curls tickling as Evan searched for Liza. Strange that she didn't greet him at the door. He glanced back at the kitchen—no dinner prepared, either.

He found her sitting silently on the bed. Pretty face forward with her focus on the window showing the street outside. Cars passed on the road, and people strolled by on the sidewalk. She was breathtakingly beautiful in the sunlight. A delicate work of art of skin and bone. Healthy and strong.

"Hello, love. Did you get out—" Words stalled in his throat. "Liza? What's wrong?"

"I met your boss today." She lowered her head and pointed her finger at the closet door. "He dropped something off for you. Said you knew what do with it. He then held Freddy and said what a handsome boy our son was."

Evan felt a cold sensation twist around his spine. A knot pulled to tighten in his gut. "Liza, I can explain."

She stood and faced him. First, she took Freddy and sat their child on the bed. Second, she slapped him so hard his lip split. "Can you, Evan? Really? How are you going to explain working for that," she began, her gaze, shimmering with angry tears, darted around the room, landing on the pressed police uniform on the doorknob of the closet, "monster? Because that's what he is! Did you honestly think I wouldn't recognize the mob boss splashed across every newspaper in town? Al Capone. Are you going to convince me you didn't know who he was?" She began to sob, her arms straight by her side. Hands curled into fists—the tightness blanching her knuckles. "You lied to me about working for some rich lawyer. You may be a driver, but if you drive that man around, you are doing more than just waiting in a car!"

"Sweetheart. I didn't know he would stop by here. I missed a meeting. But Liza, I have a reason. I've been looking for an honest, legit job, before and after Capone hired me. I had no luck until today. An interview and offer with a cab company. An actual job. Still a driver but a legal one. I negotiated to get a cut of the fare. And they're willing to lease me a cab for pennies a week." He put his hands on her arms, trying to seek her gaze, to show her that he was sincere. It would be okay. They would be fine. "I'm going to quit Capone. But Liza, don't you remember how bad it was? That shithole flat? The rats? Water so rusty that it looked like sewage rather than something we should drink?" His voice cracked with pleading. "I couldn't let you and Freddy continue to live that way. They said this depression wouldn't last, but it has. The past three years had been one thing after another. Jobs are few and far between. Especially for the Irish. No one trusts us. It doesn't matter if we were born here or not. He might be a mobster, but Capone gave me a chance. Working for him, I was able to get us out of the slums."

He motioned around them and brought his palms up between them. "It's because of him we are in this apartment. The clothes you and Freddy wear. The food we have rather than starving on scraps from the trash." A shaking hand tentatively pressed against her cheek. "Please, sweetheart, I did it to take care of my family. Did you think I didn't mean that in our vows?" Evan searched her eyes for some hint of understanding. A reflection, however minuscule, of forgiveness. "I didn't lie to you. You know I never would."

"Really, Evan?" She batted his hand away and, with angry steps, went over to the uniform to jerk it from its place. "A policeman's uniform? Are you going to tell me this, your job, is not a lie?" She laughed a pained sound. "It's almost Valentine's Day, not Halloween, Evan."

Evan squeezed his eyes tight. Palms came up to cover his face. He never imagined Capone would have visited their apartment. "I planned on telling you." His hands dropped, his back bowed in anguish. "Every day, I told myself, 'Today, I will tell Liza everything.' I just knew you'd want me to quit!" He felt desperate. It chilled him to the marrow. "I wanted to find another job. So we don't end up back in that place. Poor and broke. Like so many on the streets. Liza! Please. You need to see this from my side."

She jerked back at his words. As if they carried a blow and struck her. "Your side? How can I? I don't have it in me to see anything from the eyes of a criminal!" She pressed herself into the corner, shook her head rapidly as she angrily wiped away tears. "What does that mean?" She pointed to the uniform crumpled on the floor. "What does he have you doing, Evan?"

"Liza, I don't want to put you in danger. If he finds out you know—"

She rushed at him from the corner, palms hitting his chest to shove him back. "I don't care! Don't you think we're in danger now? He *held* our son! He was in *our* home! Tell me! No more lies!" Her hands balled up into fists to strike him over and over. Evan grabbed her wrists, and she collapsed against him. "Please. Oh god, Evan. I need to know."

Evan rested his chin on top of her head and wrapped his arms around her. There'd be no going back now. Capone had not only opened a can of bloody worms but had also fed them to Evan's wife as a truth serum. He wondered if the mob boss did it on purpose. Had the man noticed his absence some days? The times

Evan ran late to one meeting or another or turned down a demanded job or a hit? Evan knew the way Capone's sharp mind functioned. Calculations made with no facts, but gut. He must believe Evan was a traitor to the gang. That, or he worked for the cops.

His eyes went to the uniform. What if it was a "note" of Capone's assumption? Incorrect or not. More than a costume for the murderous ruse in two days? Evan dared not reveal his quest for legit employment. His intention was to quit the mob then. He'd worry about that later. Liza sobbed in his arms. His son cried on the bed, sensing his parents' unrest. They were his only priority—the mess with Capone he'd handle later.

Evan took Liza's hand and led her to the bed to sit. When she pulled Freddy into her arms, not only to soothe but hold Evan's son away from him, it smarted. She sheltered the boy with her embrace from the threat she now saw was her husband. Could he blame her? No. They both loved Freddy as much as any parents could.

"He has a job. Bugsy Malone's gang has been slowly creeping into Capone's territory. Malone keeps ambushing Capone's gin transports. Hit some of Capone's businesses and offered shop owners better deals on protection. Capone is possessive. He's tried minor tactics to end the intrusion, but none worked. He's ruthless. He's taking an extreme measure to stop Malone before it's too late."

He stood to lift the uniform from the floor. "We're going to dress like cops. Malone has so many dirty ones in his pocket there's no way he knows them all. He'll think we're some of the cops he's paid off. Then," his chin dropped to hit his chest as he exhaled slowly, "we'll gun him and his gang down. Take Malone out. Capone already knows where he will be." He didn't risk a look at Liza. He knew what he'd find—fear, shock, and worst of all, disappointment.

Evan never lied to his wife in their years of marriage. As far as he knew, neither had she. However, over the last few years, he'd done nothing but lie to her about his life outside this apartment. He religiously left work there. Never brought it here. Their home was a heavenly haven—a shelter from the bloody and stressful days of being an upper man under Capone's control.

"My saying I loved you, loved Freddy, was never a lie. And the reason I did all of it, Liza. I love you both so much that I'd do anything to take care of you." He finally looked sideways at her. "Even this. Kill, fight, rob, and threaten, if it meant the two of you lived a life worth living."

Liza's sobs renewed and became more heartbreaking. "You chose one of crime? You call that a life?" She jumped to her feet, and Freddy joined in on the crying from Liza's hip. Evan directed his focus to his son. He attempted to take him from Liza's arms, but she recoiled. "You will stop this."

"I told you I wanted a new job before I quit. Tell you every-thing. I had to make sure you two were taken care of, that I could continue to keep you both safe. And happy. Healthy and off the damn streets!"

Evan stepped up close to her, his anger ticking up by the second. Not at her, but at himself. He knew how wrong his choices had been. He ignored the guilt if it meant she and Freddy lived a better life. But with each truth spilling from Liza's mouth at his errors, self-loathing rose to devour him. Each bite was venom to his soul.

"Liza, he won't let me out of this plan. Him coming by here makes that abundantly clear. I'll do it, and then it's done. I promise."

"You expect me to believe your promises? And how can you call us safe? He was here! He knows where we live!" She searched his eyes, and she clenched her teeth. "You stop that monster's plan. You save the lives he wants to kill." She hesitated for only a moment. "Before you're one of them." She deflated with a sob and came close to trail her trembling fingers down his face. "Please,

Evan. I want the man I love to do the right thing. Because I don't recognize the man that would do what you're doing. I need us back like before. I don't care if it's on the streets or in a shelter or back in that horrible flat. At least there, I trusted you. And I knew you were an honorable man."

Her touch drifted from his face, and Evan longed for it to return. He hoped it would restore the connection they had always possessed.

Until now.

Frayed and severed because of him.

"Liza, Capone is not a man you mess with. Nor disappoint. I owe him money. Debts. He won't just let me walk away. And yes, he knows where we live. He could—"

"Hold Freddy."

Confused by her reason, he took their son. She moved away and pulled a hatbox from under the bed. "I do have horrible dreams about losing all of this. It seemed too good to be true. Maybe a woman's premonition or something." She sat on the bed and opened the box. Inside were compact bundles of money, what appeared to be shopping lists and coins. "I put away a little each time you gave me money to buy groceries. Or anything." She laughed weakly. "If us being poor taught me anything, it's how to budget. How to do a lot with a little." She lifted hopeful eyes to his and bit her lip nervously. "It's not a lot. But maybe you could give it to Capone? Tell him about your new job? Work out a way for us to pay him the rest. I'll help. I did this." She motioned to the money. "I can do it to get us out of this. We'll give up this place. Evan…" She left the box on the bed, stood, and splayed her hands on his chest. "I don't care about this place. I only care about you and Freddy. Please, stop this."

With jaw dropped, he looked from the cash to her. "You've been hiding this? You're skimming what I gave you? Because you were afraid of losing all of this?" He felt hurt at her deception. The lack of faith he'd felt sure of before. Aware it made him a hypocrite considering the distrust and deceit he expected her to forgive. "Didn't you trust me to provide for you two? I always have."

Liza released a ragged breath. Her face fell, and her eyes lowered. "I know," she said barely above a whisper. "I also knew that someday, you might need me to take care of you. I wanted to make sure I could." Her forehead fell forward to rest on his chest.

Freddy whimpered against Evan's shoulder as he sucked his thumb. Looking from him back down to Liza, he brought a hand up to cup the back of her head. "Of course you did. Because that's how love is." He tilted her chin to meet her eyes. "You do what you have to do. But unlike you, I didn't consider the cost. I'll end it. All of it. I promise."

He thought she agreed with understanding. That forgiveness was a given. He was wrong.

"I want to trust you, Evan." She pulled back and took Freddy from his hold. Her expression hardened, and she raised her chin. "I have no reason to believe you. I promise to try. But Evan..." She turned away and began to cry. Wiping her eyes, she turned to face him again. "If you don't, I'm going to leave you. I'll take our son, and I'll be gone." She walked out of the room. "And you will never see us again."

***

Evan's body shook with a deep exhale. "I should have told her. I kept telling myself I needed to. For years, miles from the fucking truth. She never questioned me." He gave Lily a look of anguish. "Liza trusted me completely, and I disrespected her on every damn level with my lies."

He stayed stiff across the room. Posture tight like a tightrope. An air of unapproachability thickening the space between them. Lily ached to go to him as he wrenched the painful story into a vocal form from memory. She longed to wrap her arms tight around him, to act as a buffer against the torment of emotions battering him. The onslaught even she felt with each sentence. She held her breath in anxious anticipation, knowing where the tale would go.

Lily knew history—the end of the story approached like a loose freight train. She considered telling him to stop, not to tell her more, and spare them both. She stayed silent. Maybe he needed to get the details of his buried past out. And she braced for the pain of the conclusion all Breakers experienced in their mortal life—death.

"The thought of losing her and Freddy. That Liza would ever leave me. I don't know why I never thought she would, no matter what I did. It was both arrogant and foolish." He swallowed, and his nostrils flared with an inhale of breath. "I begged her to stay. She made that one demand. No reasoning I gave her would change her mind. My Liza was a very stubborn woman when forced."

He gave Lily a forlorn smile. "Much like you. I had to stop Capone's plan. But how?" His neck arched, and he focused on the ceiling again. "Capone's hit was already in motion. So I did the only thing that stood a chance of preventing the goal." He leveled his eyes with hers. "I went to the enemy. Bugsy Malone. I warned him of Capone's plan. You can imagine how well they took one of Capone's top gang members showing up. They beat me. Almost to death. All while I tried to tell them. To stop the slaughter." He laughed bitterly. "They took the money that my lovely Liza saved up for our fresh start."

A ragged exhale signaled the arc of the end of his story.

"The Valentine's Day Massacre happened. I lay unconscious, left for dead in the city dump by Malone's gang. However, its leader, Bugsy Malone, got away. He decided not to take a chance if I had told the truth. But one of Capone's fatally wounded men had last words with Capone before his final breath." He slid down the wall and sat. "My name. The one who told Malone of the plan. I don't know how this man knew. Maybe he worked inside of both gangs. Not unheard of. It happens in any world. Past or present. Even ours." Evan focused on his hand, a finger tracing a deep, white, aged scar across the back. "I missed the massacre. My absence only played into what Capone was told. As I tried to get home, I was barely able to walk and passed out as I bled and stumbled. They found me on the way. Another brutal, cold massacre occurred. That one didn't make the papers." He swung a haunted gaze to hers. "Mine."

Lily's hands covered her mouth to stifle sobs. Hot tears trickled over her fingers to splatter the blanket. "Oh my god, Evan. And Liza? Freddy?"

Evan rose, head lowered, and arms wrapped around himself. "When Bounce first offered me a chance, years had gone by, though only the span of days in Hell. Human time is irrelevant there. I tried to find them, but I had no luck. It was decades later when I found any records in the San Francisco Chronicles. They were evicted from our home. Liza had no choice but to go to the women's and children's shelter. There they both became ill, succumbed to it, and were buried in a mass grave in Potter's Field." He laughed with a sob. "A death log. Elizabeth O'Brien. Two children. One three and another unborn." He sobbed more. "She was pregnant. And I didn't know. Maybe it was the reason behind her savings. I have no idea."

His voice raised in anger. "It had been for nothing. My choices, my lies, my trying to save it all, was for..." He bared his fangs, swallowed, and began to yell. "It was all for fucking nothing. So you can see why I decided never to put another person in the position I had put Liza in—to choose a job over a loved one. To ever have to decide. When you live a dangerous life, you have a target on your back. You know that as well as I do, Lily."

He met her eyes with his jaw set. The zeal of enraged determination in his gaze locked Lily's breath in her chest painfully.

"When death has you constantly in its sights, you don't put someone you love in its path."

The way he spat the words, the hardened glare he directed her way, sent a chill of apprehension up Lily's spine. The level of intensity caused the hair to rise on the back of her neck. She opened her mouth to request he clarify. Had he directed his statement at her? She didn't get a chance. Evan closed off and put his back to her. A dense, brooding silence overtook the space before he stepped under the door above them.

"We need to get out of here."

## 15

How the fuck did he allow himself to give in to his attraction to Lily Devenmore? Not only in a reckless sexual manner but a more dangerous emotional one. Her kindness honed deception and lock-picked the boxes of his past, keying into his vulnerable flaws, exposing weaknesses to exploit. And knowing Lily as he did, she would use the knowledge without batting a lovely eyelash. When he put a stop to—well, he had no idea what existed between them now. Just that he shouldn't have let it happen. Whatever *it* was.

Evan never fully understood claustrophobia. An overwhelming need to flee a room or space. The affliction could manifest with no prior history and gave no warning because he wanted out of the bunker ASAP.

He dressed in his remaining clothes quickly as Lily scrambled to find her clothes. He silently reprimanded himself for being tempted to watch her do the deed. To get one last look at all that glorious skin before she covered it up. Pretty confident he wouldn't get a chance to see it again.

Regret could wait, and he ignored her attempts to get him to talk and stop pacing. Guns in his hands, he moved back under the door to stare up at it. "This has gone on for too long. I have to end it."

She gently touched his arm. "Evan, we talked about it. You—"

"Get off of me!" he barked at her. Hurt flickered in her eyes instantly. Soured her pretty features as she stepped out of his personal space. His thoughts cleared with her touch removed. The scent of their sex was strong on her skin. Yes, he felt like shit that he had hurt her feelings. Perhaps it was for the best, considering how badly he had fumbled the situation already.

"Hello?"

Both Lily and Evan's head whipped upward. The voice came from the other side of the door. Evan brought his finger up to press over his lips. Lily nodded as he climbed the first two rungs of the ladder. Flicking the gun's safety with his thumb, he held the weapon loosely at his side and finger near the trigger. It had gone quiet above. He angled his head to try to hear any noise, eyes darting back to Lily. He couldn't be losing his mind—she had heard it too.

"Hello, are you there?"

"That's Kyle," Lily whispered from below.

Evan frowned and asked in a hushed tone, "The younger brother, right?"

Lily nodded. "The one begging on the call earlier not to die." She moved into the tunnel. "He got in trouble for talking to us. Told us he didn't do any of this. He felt bad. Apologized. I think he did it for his brother. I don't think he'd do it otherwise."

Looking upward, Evan waved a hand to instruct Lily to move back and ascended to the door. He noted a few gapping dings around the edges from the earlier attempts of the men to break in. "I hear you. What is it you want?"

A soft sliding told Evan to move over to the door to speak through the small openings. Through the slit, Evan was able to see a brown eye—wide, exhausted, and clearly, Kyle was scared. "I don't want to die. They keep calling, asking how you are. They want us to show them you're alive. Are you okay? Your girlfriend?"

"She's not my girlfriend," Evan mumbled.

Lily, at the same time, yelled upward, "I am *not* his girlfriend."

*Awkward.*

And her voice echoed in the tunnel. An echo as if he needed to hear Lily say it more than once. Evan slid the safety back on his weapon and holstered it. "We are well. Unharmed. You know what happens next, right?"

Kyle sniffed and disappeared from Evan's sight for a second and returned. "Yeah, they will get sick of this. We are going to die, aren't we?" He gasped through staggered breathing. "I don't want to die. I don't want a sniper to take us out. Can you help? This was an awful idea. I told Charlie it would go south. But he never listens to me. And now—" The man let out such a deep sigh, Evan heard it. "Now he wants to die. Charlie wants your people to kill him. He doesn't want to go to jail again. I don't want to go, either, but dying to get out of it seems as stupid as the rest of this."

Evan hoped headquarters knew he and Lily were in the substation. Both alive and well. The man's statements confirmed the opposite if negotiations continued. Or perhaps a stall to get the brothers to surrender. Evan rubbed his forehead before letting it rest on the ladder rung in front of it. He was so exhausted. A shower and a monster style In-N-Out burger with hot string fries sounded like heaven to him. His gaze slid down to Lily as she returned to stand under the tunnel. She chewed a fingernail and had a hopeful look of anticipation that he had a plan.

He didn't. Not even a hint of one but no need to tell her that. *You've told her plenty already.* Apparently, building a craving for a messy burger deal led to personal life word vomit.

He squeezed his eyes shut. He took a few beats to think. *Plan. Come on. You're a leader for a reason. You call the shots now. So call a damn—*

His head shot up. "Listen to me, Kyle. I can end this *without* you or your brother dying. But you have to help me. Can I trust you do that?"

Evan's inquiry was met with silence. He feared Kyle had changed his mind. Worse, was forming a trap with his brother.

"How do I know I can trust you not to kill us? I guess we're in the same spot."

He gave him credit for that correct analysis. "Fine. Here's what I need you to do. There's a walk-in cooler that hides the entrance you're in. I need you to slide it back in place. It's on tracks. You should be able to do it quietly. Once you do that, I'll take care of the rest. I vow not to kill you and do my best about your brother. But I don't want to die any more than you, understood?" He wasn't sure he could keep the last part of the vow. When a person decided to die by cop or foe, past experiences taught Evan, more times than not, the person would do whatever steps it took to make it happen.

"Evan!" Lily hissed as loud as a whisper could go. "Speaking of promises made of bullshit, didn't you promise to wait for nighttime??" She tugged on his jeans leg, her expression and voice pleading, "What if that's a trick? A total set-up? I thought you had a *brain!*"

Growling in frustration, he dropped to the floor to stand in front of her. "Do you have any other plans? If it's a set-up, do you honestly think I can't take two humans?" He smirked. "We both know I can. Or we can wait until snipers take out both men and two lives are lost, which will make things messy for Bounce and the Grid. Does that sound better to you? Because to me, it sounds less than desirable."

He just *had* to use the word desirable. His recent lust-filled brain and desire-sated body reacted as if Lily had licked each letter of the word on his cock. It hardened behind his fly at the thought of her using linguist skills on the shaft, flicking her tongue to spell out different and longer words. Like *supercalifrag-ilisticexpialidocious*, role-playing a sexy Mary Poppins. Complete with a spoon full of sugar that had *nothing to* do with the granular stuff.

"Just slide the machine back where it goes? That's it?"

Evan exhaled with relief upon hearing Kyle's return and climbed up the ladder to respond. "That simple. I'll know when you've completed it. Do *not* tell your brother. You do, chances are I can't keep my vow. You both might die."

"Okay," the man said before Evan heard footsteps across the door as they moved away. Evan hopped down, and a few seconds later, the systems came back online. Next, he felt the buzz of his stamp. "Perfect." Moving past Lily, he went over to the communication system, hoping more juice overrode the damage. "Shit. Still dead."

He touched his stamp, but static filled his head. They were underground, surrounded by up to six inches of steel. Not to mention the store and police equipment above creating signal inference. Without the radio transmitter to increase the strength, they had no such luck reaching HQ.

"Evan, think about it. You're trusting a criminal. For all we know, killers with zero eth—" Lily must have realized how her words hit sideways. Her mouth snapped shut as she reached to take his hand. "I didn't mean that toward you. They are nothing like you, Evan."

He pulled his hand from her, bristling. "Like me now. But very much as I used to be."

A pinging noise filled the space behind him, and he glanced over his shoulder to find the blur point pad had flickered. After a few moments, the illumination remained steady as it went online. "Perfect."

"Oh, thank god. We can leave. I've needed to poop since we woke up."

Evan stared at her. Of all the things she could say.

She shrugged. "What? Girls never poop around guys. Especially ones they had sex with. It ruins the glamour of it all." She crossed her arms with a sarcastic smile. "Are you telling me you find the image of me squatting on the toilet appealing?" She dropped her arms to wave a hand around. "I didn't think so."

"You boggle me so often. It makes me dizzy." He took Lily's arm in his hand and led her to the blur point. "I'm getting you out of here."

"Me?" Lily jerked her arm away and shoved them both from the pad. "No. *We.* You used the word wrong there. And trust me, words are my thing." A blink after she shoved him, she hauled him to her. Her arms wrapped him in a hug, cheek pressed against his chest, and she whispered, "We, Evan. Say *we* are getting out of here."

He brought a hand up, smoothed it over her hair and lowered his head to kiss the crown of hers. "We are blurring out of here, Lily."

She tilted upward to meet his eyes, and a tearful smile spread on her pretty face. "There. Was it *that difficult* to agree with me?"

He returned the smile and wiped the tears betraying her fear. "No, but I wouldn't expect it often." Dipping his head down, he meshed his mouth with hers in a kiss and blurred them both.

"Look, we have to know how our people are. Beth, can you please talk some sense to these damn people?" Jess was pissed. Also tired, cranky, hungry, and starting to need a bath something awful real soon. "I'd also like to point out the wrong bullet in the wrong place may make our armory of kill-em toys go boom. And that means you lose this whole damn block." He looked around and back. "And a whole lot of people."

Beth demanded the attention of the deputy chief of San Fran with attitude and defiance to plead their case. Associated with the Grid, the man knew of the supernatural options, but the fact the site bustled with non-Grid personnel made those a no-go. Press flocked at the wings, and spectator looky-loos watched the action. All it lacked was the popcorn and Big Gulp cups of soda. The whole situation was a powder keg ready to blow if the wrong fuse was lit. Having snipers in the process of setting up on the roofs across from the store didn't help defuse it one bit.

"Chief, we're asking for a few more hours. We already pulled the other hostages out. We just want time to get our two people out of there." Beth glanced over at Jess and he got a glimpse of the glare directed at the deputy. The type shriveling normal-sized man balls—which his weren't. Aesthetics were important with his

Wrangler fly parts to be a matching trio of manly impressiveness. He also found her cop-itude hot as hell and hoped the deputy chief didn't have a wife. And if she did, he wouldn't object to her husband coming home nut-less.

"Sir, ignore Woody, but Detective Bailey is correct," Reznor stated in an attempt to help. Jess had to give the man credit. Both Maine and his woman were debriefed and cleared to leave but stayed to help. "Time would be appreciated while we—"

"Lily!"

Desi's squeal interrupted Reznor when the woman took off running. Jess pivoted as every armed person brought up their guns in alarm. At the cause of Desi's excitement, he motioned for them to lower their weapons. "What the hell?"

Evan and Lily stepped out of the mobile command center.

"Let me guess." Reznor moved to stand next to him. "He pulled off more of that supernatural A and B magic?"

Desi reached the couple first and threw her arms around Lily. "Jesus, you had us so worried! Are you okay?" She pulled back and regarded Evan. "And you do look like Ryan Reynolds. You were right, Lily." She looked backward over her shoulder at Jess and Reznor. "Be glad you're lucky I choose you, Rez, or you'd have some competition." She giggled. "And I would be spending more time in San Francisco." She hugged Lily a second time. "You were holding back on me. All these fine men where you work." She smiled. "And the cool supernatural stuff." She leaned in to whisper, "I signed the NDA. I don't think it covers—"

"It does cover girl talk. Sorry, darlin'." Jess hung back bent at the waist to put his hands on his knees and blew out a breath. "Damn." Evan looked a bit worse for wear. Lily looked healthy and whole.

Joining them, he paused and narrowed his eyes as he skimmed over a mark on Lily's neck. Fang marks. A bite. Raising a brow, he swung his focus over to Evan with a grin. "Oh, well, I guess *someone* was havin' an enjoyable time while the rest of us were crapping our drawers to save them. Enjoy your meal?"

"What?" Desi leaned closer and openly pointed out what Jess hadn't yet. "Oh, is that a hickey?"

Evan flustered, Lily blushed, and Jess brought a hand up to give himself a facepalm. "Well, it ain't a bullet hole, that's for sure." Jess tapped a finger on his fangs. "It's part of the appeal."

Desi broke out in laughter. Good thing she *had* signed a Grid NDA, too. She hauled Reznor in to show him off to Lily. "Rez, Lily. Lily, my man Rez." She nudged her boyfriend with an elbow before switching gears to address Evan. "Will you be joining us as Lily's plus one when we go to dinner? I really think you should."

Beth joined Jess, but she didn't look nearly as entertained as he was watching the two couples.

"Dinner is going to have to wait." She crossed her arms. "We have a problem."

Jess turned his head in regard and waved a hand at Evan and Lily. "How? They're out."

Beth sighed. "Yeah, and they now have no reason not to use the snipers." She crossed her arms. "The two men have stopped answering the phone. And now that they know about the substation. There's too much risk if they reach it. They are going hot to take the kill shots in thirty."

Reznor let out a string of curse words as he looked toward the early morning sky. "Guess negotiation is over."

*L*ily's friend continued to babble, but Evan focused on the surrounding activity. Moving past the others, he regarded the storefront. "I made a vow."

Jess came to stand next to him. "You and Lily, huh? That's surprising. And vow? Did you two get hitched in there?" He snorted. "I don't think it counts if you perform the deed yourself without a preacher. I think Bounce can ordain. He'll be shocked too. You might wish you had stayed in that bunker."

Evan shook his head. "No. I made a vow to one brother that if he assisted in our escape, I would save them both. Prevent what is about to happen"—he glanced at his watch—"in twenty-three minutes."

Jess shrugged. "You did what you could. They're refusing to answer the phone. Ain't a lot we can do. They won't come out. They won't surrender, and they won't help us help them." The cowboy brought a hand up to clap on Evan's shoulder. "It's sad and all. But take it from a former gunslinger who faced off a posse more than once, death is usually the outcome when you ain't trying to do anything but die."

"Only one of them wants to die. I won't let that happen." Walking back to the command center, Evan removed his tactical gear, dumping it and his guns on the bench. "I'm going in there. Blur in, immobilize the one brother and get them both out." He turned his head to see Jess stood in the doorway. "Alive. Tell your wife to inform the police that if they snipe the place, they risk hitting me. I'd rather that didn't happen. I have a 'getting shot once a day' rule." He checked his wound and found it still bleeding. He tugged his soiled shirt off and re-bandaged it as he dug for a clean black tee from the supply cabinet. Both men in the store wore black. The low light of morning would make it harder to distinguish Evan from the brothers, making it difficult for a sniper to determine a target. Or so Evan hoped. Even an immortal couldn't survive a nicely placed headshot.

"I see Lily gives as good as she gets, huh?" Jess pointed with a grin at Evan's chest. He looked down in confusion to discover what Cowboy found worthy of comment. His chest and abs were marked with deep scratches. Jess was intelligent enough to know they were *not* self-inflicted. Evan grunted to indicate there wouldn't be an additional comment on the subject as he pulled the tee on and jumped out of the trailer. "Off-limits, Bailey."

"Off Lily? You claiming her?" Jess walked beside him. "You ain't got to worry. Been there and done that. Then married a cop who would shoot me in the dick if I cheated. If I even wanted to. But E, damn, bit over twenty-four hours, and you've stamped her as yours and no one else's. I'm real proud of yo—"

"Shut up." Evan bunched Bailey's shirt in his hands and roughly slammed him against the command trailer. "Lily and I had sex. It meant zero. It changes nothing. And it is not something I want spoken of again. Understood?"

"So you're ashamed? Embarrassed?" Lily asked in a voice full of raw hurt behind Evan's back.

"Shit," both he and Jess said at the same time. Evan's head dropped forward to rest on his hands, still fisting Bailey's shirt.

"Lily." He sighed, let Jess go, and he turned to face her. "That's not what I meant. Not at all."

"Really? Do you think you're the first guy not to find me

worth anything more than a way to pass the time? The difference with you is we did it without clothes. In a stupid bunker. With our lives at risk. Shot at." She brought a hand up and pointed at Jess. "Ask him. He did it. Yeah, I was so desperate for love, I made the mistake of sleeping with my sister's hand-me-down ex."

"Hey, that makes me sound like an unwanted casserole."

"Shut up!" Both Evan and Lily yelled at the cowboy. Jess, in turn, had the sense enough to step away and leave Evan with Lily, undoubtedly to argue, having been in a position similar to Evan.

Waiting until others knew to give the two of them space, Evan blew out a frustrated breath and put his hand on Lily's arm. "I am not ashamed. Nor am I embarrassed for others to know what we did. I enjoyed it. You enjoyed it. But after hearing my story, surely you understand why I will *not* choose between my duty and a relationship." He brushed his knuckles over the bite mark on her neck. "I shouldn't have allowed my desire for you to override my sense."

Lily slapped his hand away and stepped into his space. "Your sense? Really? You cannot *tell* me it didn't mean something to you! And I am not talking about sex." She swallowed and angrily wiped tears—no doubt welled from anger—before she pointed a finger against his chest. "The fact you told me about your past should tell you something. And the way you spoke about me, how you wanted me, there was no sense to it. You, wanting someone like me. That was so much more than sex. If it were only sex, you would not have felt open enough to tell me about your past." She snorted and stabbed her finger once more. Evan was sure she wanted to pierce his heart with it. "Or do you share your deepest regrets and shames as a form of some weird afterglow with all your lovers?"

Evan wrapped his fingers around her wrist to pull her hand from him. "No. You would be the first. Take some comfort in that, Lily." He attempted to step away from her.

"Comfort? Are you kidding me?" She slapped him so hard

that he tasted blood. "You are a coward. Do you hear me, Evan O'Brien? A complete and total coward!"

He moved to the opposite side, managed to get away only for her to grab his shirt and spin him back to her. "Just like you were a chicken to tell Liza. You're just as scared to love me. To even *try!*"

Evan hissed a snarl. God, the woman knew how to push his buttons. And he'd given her shiny new ones to pound. "I am not a coward. Not anymore. And the heartache with Liza is the *exact* reason there is zero chance of there being anything more between you and me. You think with your heart. You let it call all your shots. And that's admirable. Brave. However, I function and decide with my head. My brain. My heart has no place in my existence. And as long as this war continues, that will not change." He gently tugged her hand from his shirt. "It is not personal against you, that I can swear to you, Lily. Now excuse me, I have a vow to keep."

"Vow?" She suddenly realized he no longer wore his tactical gear, which led to her recalling the vow he made to Kyle. She paled. "You are going back in there? But you said *we* were escaping! Did you lie? Is that what the honorable Evan O'Brien does? Color me surprised. I've learned *so* much about you during this brief adventure."

"I did not lie!" He roared at her. They were running out of time. The more she said, the crappier he felt about himself and how wrong he had handled the fallout of what they'd done. He *really* needed to focus on the upcoming hail Mary move. "I said we'd blur out. And we did. I did *not* say I wouldn't go back in there."

Lily gasped and took a clumsy step back. "You got me out of the way. You tricked me? Evan! Why?" She came close to him again. "Did you use me? No, you wouldn't do that. I cannot believe you are that type, E. Tell me you aren't."

Putting his head back, Evan shook it slowly. "No. It is my job to keep you and others on the Grid safe. As far as what happened between us? Isn't it you that said the past doesn't stay with us?" His eyes dropped to hers. "And what happened to us is just that. The past and there is nothing beyond it." He side-stepped and called back, "It's not personal, Lily."

He didn't hear what else she had to say. There was a small window of under fifteen minutes before two men, criminals or not, would meet a death sentence for their deeds. He heard her rushing steps behind him, catching up. He looked up to see Jess by the trailer. He growled as he passed. "Stop her. I don't have time for the drama."

Jess gave him an acknowledging nod and moved to cut off Lily's path. Evan glanced back to see Jess place himself in front of the woman. She turned her verbal tirade on the cowboy. Opening the trailer, he slammed the door behind him, walked over to the blur point, closed his eyes, and disappeared.

---

"Jess! Move, dammit!"

Lily cried, pled, and blathered. She wasn't even sure why. A mixture of anger, frustration, and fear rolled into one blubbering mess. Atypical female behavior—something Lily detested. Jess held her arms in his hands, a big, muscle wall of a man obstructing her way. She could only watch helplessly over Jess's shoulder as Evan entered the trailer. If she reached it, she'd now find it empty. Blurs didn't take much time. A blink and poof. Someone there one moment. The next, only air left behind.

Air would be nice. She didn't feel like she had any to exhale. Incapable of inhaling. Her chest malfunctioned on some anatomical, cellular level. She went to her haunches, and Jess followed. Lily tried to focus on his face. Couldn't he see how she felt?

"You're supposed to be on my side, Princess." A name she hadn't called Jess since she was a teen. She felt as vulnerable now as she did then. Maybe using it would remind him whose friend he was supposed to be. She sobbed, "He's going back in there unarmed. He's going to die for men undeserving of that sacrifice, Jess." She clutched the lapels on his leather jacket in her hands. "Please. Go after him. Stop him. Give him backup or do something?" She looked past him, and the door stayed closed. Evan had left. How could it be possible she *felt* him leave? "Please. Why aren't you doing something, Jess?"

"Darlin', Lily, listen to me."

He cupped her face in his big, warm hands. Lily usually found calm in Jess's gentle strength in the worst moments of her life. But not this time. She met his whiskey brown eyes, crumbled, and felt Jess's solid arms wrap tight around her to prevent her from falling to the ground.

"Shh, darlin'. Lily, he's going to be fine. Evan always is. He knows what he's doing." Jess angled back to brush her tears away and tucked locks of hair behind her ears. "Evan's probably as good if not better than me." Jess smiled. "And if you ever tell him that, I'll kick your delightful ass."

Lily would have laughed before. Jess's humor was a thing of wonder in the most awful of situations. One of his many charms. But not this time. Maybe she was having a heart attack. How could Evan doing his job mess her up this bad? It had to be on account of something else. She had eaten little but old MREs and drank water that might or might not have expired—if water could expire. And other than a few hours of sleep after patching up Evan and a few more in his arms when they…

And cue the waterworks again.

"Damn, Lily, you got it bad."

Jess's words were simple. She wanted to deny them—each individual letter of the entire statement. But then she would be the one lying. Why fight it? She had feelings for Evan down to her soul's core. Perhaps the temptation to anger or frustrate him as much or as often as she had was a fragile coping mechanism, a way to avoid acknowledging what might be a growing love. She stood with Jess keeping an arm around her waist. She leaned against him, speaking against his shirt. "I do. I don't understand how it happened. But I saw a different side of him. And there's so much more to him, Jess." He gently moved her back, tugged his shirttail up and gently wiped her face.

"Yeah, most of us have more to us. It just takes a hell of a lot for us to show it." Finished with the cleaning, even letting her blow her nose, he gave her an understanding smile. "But unfortunately, we develop handy honed skills of putting it back from where it came from. Eventually, we forget how to even reach it. We go on with our day-to-day, knowing it lurks under the surface of who we are. Little bubbles of emotional air making us pause, see if it becomes a wave, and wanting at the same time as not wanting to drown it. But eventually, the air runs out. We hope it's dead. Held to the bottom of our own wells of sorrow, never to rise again. It works. For a time." He brushed his fingers over her cheek. "But then we realize it's all we have left of being human. Without it, we're just a barren sea."

Taking her hands in his, Jess bent down to meet her eyes. "But Lily, you can't fault him for wanting it to stay that way. Locked down, sealed up and put away. A man or, hell, a woman does that for so long, and then it's all they know. They no longer recognize the person they used to be—just another stranger of no consequence. There's comfort in that. E ain't no different."

Lily sniffed and leaned in to rest her forehead on his broad chest. "I hate alpha males. I really do. Alpha means idiot: all brawn and no brains. I should petition Webster to put it in the dictionary. Next to a picture of Evan." Evan chose not to have a heart. Jess had changed from the alpha definition. It started when her sister Emma gave birth to his daughter, Sophia. And the evolution made full circle when a certain badass police detective came into his life. She knew that Beth and Jess both fought their attraction—only sex, nothing more. But love didn't care about the rules put on a relationship. It ripped up Bailey's foolish no-strings-attached agreement.

The difference with Evan was he forced his heart to be ancient stone, not to allow Lily, or any woman, access to its softer, beating core. *It's not personal…*

Then why did it feel so damned personal? Lily felt paralyzed with dread that she'd never get the chance to ask him.

**1 8**

van reappeared in the substation to hear screaming up above in the store. Teleporting felt strange and disorienting, but coming unarmed skyrocketed both sensations. He patted himself out of habit to check his weapons, knowing full well he had none. He could access the armory built in the wall behind him now that the systems were online. But going in armed might defeat his plan. Sucking in a huge breath, he closed his eyes to whisper, "You can do this, O'Brien. You have to."

There'd only been one other time in his life he'd put himself in such a risky position. To go in. To talk. Attempt to change events barreling down on him as fast as any bullet. The last time had been before Valentine's Day. Evan prayed this second time didn't have the same conclusion. "I'm in." He touched his stamp and knew they would monitor. Evan wrote most of the protocol of engagement. If they read his vital signs end or a fatal injury given, the plan failed. He might die, but the two men definitely would. He sent up a second prayer that Lily wouldn't be among the witnesses or hear when he went down.

Doing a cross over his chest, because an Irish Catholic he would always be, he loosened up by rolling his head, shook his arms, and then climbed the tunnel stairs. The door overhead remained locked. He keyed in the code and heard the muffled sound of the lock disengage. Sliding the door open slowly, he crouched in the narrow space behind the cooler. His fingers instinctively twitched to his sides, where holsters weren't strapped. For a century, they'd been there.

*"Please, Evan. I want the man I love to do the right thing. Because I don't recognize the man that would do what you're doing. I need us back like before. I don't care if it's on the streets or in a shelter or back in that horrible flat. At least there, I trusted you. And I knew you were an honorable man."*

Liza's voice whispered in his mind. Ironic that while the images of her pretty face faded, the recall of their last day remained vividly untouched. Time was a bitch like that.

*"You are going back in there? But you said we were escaping! Did you lie? Is that what the honorable Evan O'Brien does?*

Lily's voice chased that of Liza's ghost away. Maybe both women were right. He only found honor by doing his job better than anyone. It became a well-worn skin. Without the duty and the purpose, he'd be left raw and exposed. Strap him with guns and daggers, send him into battle, he lived for that. He even looked forward to it. Love? *That* was his greatest fear. And Lily had seen it. She was the only one that took the time to. And within the same fucking day, she threw it back in his face to wound him. He knew it would happen. Add psychic to his supernatural abilities.

Pausing behind the cooler, Evan leaned in to hear the two men still fighting. He could hear their raised voices but couldn't make out their words. Sliding the entry open, the second it yawned wide enough for him to pass into the store, a gunshot rang out to strike it. Glass shattered, and Evan threw his arms out to the side.

"Wait, I'm not armed. I'm here to help. You can shoot me, and I can guarantee the next two bullets flying will be from snipers who have you in their sights as we waste fucking time."

He met the eyes of the one in charge, Charlie.

"I get it. You want a way out. You don't care how." Evan slid his eyes to the younger brother. "Are you so sure that's what your brother wants?"

"Please, bro, listen to him. Let him help. I don't want to die."

Charlie decked his brother with a vicious punch. It sent Kyle crashing into a rack of chips. Evan remained unmoving, in position as Charlie stepped to him. Anger mottled the man's face, glazed his eyes.

"Fuck you. It's you and that bitch's fault! We had more to negotiate with before you helped the others escape. And then the bullshit of you hiding in the fucking basement like rats? You think that was helping us? No."

Charlie raised the gun and pressed it against Evan's forehead. Evan didn't bat an eye or flinch, just continued to meet the man's glare and calmly responded. "Agreed. Which brought me here to assist." He didn't disclose the deal he had made with Kyle. That would escalate the situation beyond repair. "You have little time. In fifteen minutes, give or take a few, those snipers will put a bullet in your head. And in your brother's. Yet, I am here to stop that from happening. You can either take my help or not. I can watch your bodies hit the floor. See your blood splatter the shelf of Little Debbies, eat an oatmeal pie, which is my favorite by the way, and carry on with my day." He shrugged. "I tried. You denied that help, and that's not on me, Charlie." He dropped his arms. "I won't lose any sleep over your deaths. But you and your brother would sleep forever. If you can call death sleep."

"Charlie..." Kyle came up to stand alongside his brother. "Please. I know you don't want to go back to jail. But do you want to die? I don't." He reached up and carefully pushed his brother's arm down to lower the gun. "Let's see what he can do. At least listen? Let's see how he can help. Okay?"

Charlie hissed through his teeth, turned around, and let out a roar. Well, crap, they were all about to make a big mess of blood and gore on the floor.

*Good plan, Evan. Lousy execution—literally.*

But then, Charlie's fingers loosened on the gun as he turned back to Evan. "Fine. Let's hear how you think we can make this less of a clusterfuck."

---

"Java."

Lily glanced over at Beth and then to the paper cup of coffee she had placed on the ground next to her. This nightmare hit another day. A final one. She hadn't been able to listen long to the live feed of what transpired inside the store. She felt like screaming. She was painfully tensed, waiting for a shot. For Evan's stamp to go dead as he did. Her heart couldn't take it, and she knew it.

"Thanks." Taking the coffee, she transferred her attention back to the store. "He's an idiot. What kind of man walks into danger like that with no weapons? No vest. Nothing." She let out a sad chuckle. "The man doesn't even wear underwear." Sipping on the coffee, Lily sighed. "For years, I've had feelings for Evan. I also knew it was useless to have them. He has a rep. Before he became Bounce's, I guess, general person, he slept around a lot. I used to hear stories from other women on the Grid about sharing a night with him. I also heard some of them pissed when he didn't even look their way the next day. As if the time with them meant nothing to him." She laughed. "It probably didn't. Just like I don't matter to him now." She set the cup down and brought her hands up to cover her face. "I called him a coward for not giving us a chance. But I'm no better. I crushed on him for years and was too chicken to do anything about it. To tell him." Her hands fell to her lap. "The thought of him dismissing me because of how I look, who I am… I avoided it. Better to have a crush on a guy you know you can never have than letting them know, and they crush your heart by confirming it."

"Jess had that same history," Beth said softly with a slight smile. "Oh, that's right, you would know that." She reached over to pat Lily's knee. "It's okay. He told me everything, and it was before we became a couple. A man like him *would be* a Stetson-wearing slut puppy." She sat next to Lily against a police sedan. "The tactic of throwing yourself into a job to avoid emotional pain is not an exclusive one to those in your world. We do it in mine just as much. Take me, for instance. After Dad died, and they diagnosed Mom with Alzheimer's, I worked longer hours, obsessive to move up the chain from being a beat cop. Anything and everything to escape the reality waiting for me when I took off my shield after a shift. Too exhausted, or so I told myself, to watch my mother decline." She looked forward, and Lily glanced over to watch Beth's eyes search out her husband. "I could have easily gone down the mindless, faceless sex route to deal with Mom's condition and losing my father. Instead, I put that energy into my job."

"Like Evan now," Lily whispered as she picked up the cup to fidget with the paper lip of it. "He switched from sex to work when he got promoted."

Beth nodded. "Jess did both. I think it led to his brain deteriorating when it did. He wasn't listening to all the signs, neglecting himself, refusing to see how he could continue that pace for only so long. He was on fire, burning out, and he denied the smell of the smoke. To even see the flames."

Lily remembered that. It was only a few years ago when they almost lost Jess. Luckily he was saved, enabling him to win Beth's heart—even if she wanted to shoot him daily.

"I don't want Evan to be on the brink of death to realize what he needs to be happy."

"Even if it means it's not you that he finds that happiness with?"

Beth's question hit Lily hard. When Evan was telling his story, she wanted him to find happiness with or without her. But did she mean that? Even to herself? Unable to form an answer, confused about how to spin her emotions, she held a breath. Then a second one until honesty found its way in.

"I'd be jealous as hell. Hate her without knowing her. Avoid seeing them together. Most likely try to slip carbs into every bite the bitch took. Even out the odds."

Beth bumped shoulders with her. "You know those are the actions of a woman in love, right?"

"No! Me in love with—" But how could Lily deny it? Even as she and Beth spoke, Lily kept her eyes locked on the place where Evan might have died. Did she know? No, because she sat there beyond finding out to spare herself some heartache. To not hear him die. She knew she'd feel it just as clear as she had when he blurred. Love had a signal needing no tech to work.

Did Beth stay out of it when Jess hovered at death? Did Emma give up hoping Reno would return to her even after he died?

"No, they didn't," she mumbled. Jumping to her feet, she nodded. "Right. You know what, I don't need Evan O'Brien's permission to love him. I can do that on my own. It's up to him to accept or not. Screw him and that giant stick up his ass."

"There's that stubbornness I've heard about," Beth said with a whoop as Lily ran back to the command center.

"That's insane. What makes you think they'll go along with any plan of yours?" Charlie regarded Evan with doubtful speculation. "Who the fuck are you?"

Time was ticking away fast until the two men would die. Evan received updates from Jess and Beth randomly via his stamp as they fought to buy him precious more minutes. Charlie put up one roadblock after another after hearing the plan. Scrubbing a hand over his face, Evan looked to the side. He had to get them moved past the standstill. He came up with only one way to answer and to perhaps pacify their doubts in his ability to manage the outcome, as discussed. Use both a lie and the truth. "I'm a police commander. That impressive show of force is under my command."

Charlie lost his shit and rushed Evan, slamming him back against the coolers. "I should kill you. Right now."

"Hey! Dude, he came in here with no cop gear. No gun, nothing! Why would he do that if he didn't want to help! And if he's in charge"—Kyle lowered his voice, hope having made it high-pitched—"he can tell those snipers not to take the shot." He pointed to Evan. "That's right, isn't it?"

"Yes. It is. But I am on a time limit. If we're going to do this, we do it now."

The two men debated and shoved. Evan knew to remain quiet. His eyes moved to the front of the store. It was daylight outside. The morning crept by. The sun climbed higher. It caused Evan's skin to prickle—an ingrained warning alarm at sunlight.

"I'm doing this for him."

Charlie's voice snapped him out of his butt-hurt, bruised-ego mental-whining. Didn't matter. Lily was better off without him. She must have realized it too. Liza taught him that a job with the mob and this one now with the Grid were no place for another person. It wasn't fertile ground for any kind of relationship to grow. Danger tangled, weeded it up, and brought about a withering death. The current situation proved that to be fact. "Him?"

Charlie pointed to Kyle, and for the first time, Evan saw a semblance of affection between the two men. "He's my little brother. We've only had each other until he got married. Now they're having a baby. It's my fault he quit school and can't get a decent job. He took care of everything when I got sent away. When Mom died, he paid for it all. I blew the insurance money. And I'm why he can't support his family. This was all my idea— one job to give him a big lump of cash to start things right. And no, I don't want to die. You probably don't get this, but I feel like a failure. And I'm tired of that. I'm just tired of fucking up."

"I should have told you no," Kyle said with regret. "We were just desperate, man." Swallowing as he turned to Evan. "You ever been so desperate you would do anything?"

Evan nodded. "I have. And it cost me everything." He reached out to put a hand on each man's shoulder. "Let's not let that happen to you." He smiled. "A baby needs a father he or she can count on. You don't want to learn that too late." He turned to face the front of the store. "Let's make sure you don't."

"WHAT THE HELL IS HE DOING?" Jess stood next to Lily and crossed his arms. "Huh."

She frowned in confusion. "What?" Lily shielded her eyes with a hand to see in the late morning light. Evan placed himself in front of Charlie and Kyle to block any shots, and they were walking toward the store's exit. "Jess, the sun."

The sun had begun to set, but there was ample sunlight pouring through the front windows to reach the interior of the store still. Light Evan approached the edge of. She couldn't tell if the gunmen forced him to act as a shield, or he did it on his own. Part of some crazy-ass plan she hadn't bothered to give him a chance to explain—even if he would have.

"I can't watch this. I can't. I thought I could. But if he wants to be a moron, fine. I don't have to see it." She began crying again. Dammit. Turning, she jerked her arm free of Jess's grasp as he tried to stop her and broke into a run. A contradicting heart and head made her gait more of a drunk stumble than a sleek retreat.

"Lily! Where are you going?" Desi cut off her escape, and Lily shook her head.

"I need to go, Desi. Please move." Her chest hurt. Maybe she had been right about the heart attack. There was no way it broke at the thought of Evan dying. Of never giving him hell again. Not arguing just for fun. Giving up her personal challenge to rattle the man. Damn him for taking it away from her. Screw him more than she had for taking himself away from her.

Desi reached out to rub her hand on her arm. "Lily, you know you don't want to go. You're going to have to trust your man."

"He's not my man! You honestly think he'd want me?" She threw her hand out to point to Reznor by the command trailer. "We don't all get the hero. We aren't all like you, Desi. And I'm tired of trying." Before Desi could say more, Lily was back in motion. She rushed past the police, ducked under the yellow tape, pulled her keys out of her pocket, and reached her SUV still in the parking lot across from the shopping center. Lily cried so hard that her vision blurred. Her fingers shook so badly that she dropped her keys. "God dang it. I just want to go!" Scooping up the keyring, she managed to open the door somehow and fell into the driver's seat. She took out her dread-fueled rage on the steering wheel. She turned on the radio only for it to become the next target when it played the news—coverage of the damn robbery.

"That man. God! Love him? Right! He doesn't deserve it! He doesn't deserve me! He—" But the sobbing took over, and she lost it. "Why couldn't I..." Hiccup. Sob. Sniff. More sobbing as she sputtered through her bawling, "Be a lesbian. Or a nun. Or fuck, anyone but me?"

***

"What are we waiting for? I thought we didn't have a lot of time?"

Evan had ordered both men to stay behind him, and Charlie got jumpier by the second. Evan's need to stall didn't make their freaking out any better. The mid-morning sun seemed to take its time reaching where he needed it to be. He swore it mocked him by refusing to do it's simple, before the beginning of time, job. With his arms out, he hoped to block a sniper's view of the two brothers. Both were anxious and stressed. "Stay still. Or they'll see you." Shadows crept slowly across the parking lot from the building across the street. Almost, damn you, sun, keep doing what you do. Move...

His attention shifted from the shadows when a movement beyond the cop cars caught his eye.

It was her. Lily. She stood there, wringing her hands in worry. The sunlight made her hair shine and her skin glow. He let his mind enjoy the memory of how soft it had been under his fingers. Beneath his lips. How warm and delicious she had tasted on his tongue. He couldn't fathom Lily not knowing how incredibly lusciously beautiful she was. God, he wanted to be the man to teach her to see herself as he did. He longed to lie with her in a bed instead of on a dusty cot or floor. To whisper how amazing he found each curve of her body, each dip and swell. To tell her he was falling in love with—wait, was she walking away? Holy shit, she was. He stood there, risking his life after rescuing all the hostages and saving her. Putting his ass on the line to see to her survival. Not to mention he rocked her world and worshiped her, never mind if that had been her idea… She walked away as if done with him as much as he led her to believe he was with her.

"Unbelievable." He hissed. Now he knew how all those women in one-night stands felt when shown the door at dawn. He told himself it was for the best. This situation solidified that belief. Losing his focus on matters of life or death by a woman, even one as arousing and entertaining as Lily Devenmore, could get someone killed.

"Focus, Evan," he mumbled to himself.

The moment the sunlight on the floor receded, he took slow steps to follow right behind it. Evan yelled, "We're coming out." The sun dipped lower, and Evan could then reach the door. He froze when the muzzle of Charlie's gun pressed against the small of his back. Did the idiot actually let Evan get this far, this close, only to flip a death wish? Maybe Charlie had bluffed both his brother and Evan into believing he no longer wanted to die by cop, only to reach the point so he could?

"No tricks. You better be right about this, or I'm pulling this trigger on my way to the floor. Got it?"

Relief flooded Evan, and he replied with a single nod, "Loud and clear."

---

"HERE THEY COME!" Jess yelled into the walkie, and the cops gathered behind him. He glanced back when he heard the sound of dozens of weapons being locked and loaded. He mumbled as he faced forward. "Any of you boys shoot me, we're all going to be in a world of hurt." Beth stood next to him with her gun ready.

Jess? Nah. He trusted Evan's crazy-ass plan—having eaves-dropped on the heart-to-heart as it took place in the store. Real handy tech being able to do that.

Looking up, he saw the members of SWAT on the roof of the store and locked eyes with Reznor Maine. The man offered to run point with his former squad. He'd give the Sunnyville officer a gold star for participation if no one died at the end of this rodeo. "Stay cool, fellas."

Stepping away, Jess advanced toward Evan, who crafty as a young fox, stopped short of the bright sun in the parking lot. Reaching the three men, he gave Evan a tilt of his head. "You good?" Jess leaned to the side, and he curled his lip with scorn. "You're real lucky he's helping you. I'd do it by sending your asses to an early grave. I don't take lightly to anyone even thinking about putting my wife in danger." Evan knew once the cowboy got a close up look at the two men, he would see the two men were barely old enough to grow nut hair. That Beth hadn't been in any real danger. Jess must have had a few robberies go south back in the day—perhaps he never got caught.

Jess reached into his back pocket and pulled out two sets of zip-tie cuffs, swaying them in the air as he smiled. "Now, you two be good little crooks, and let's get this over nice and easy."

Angling around Evan, Jess then saw the gun pressed against Evan's back. Snapping his eyes to the fella holding it, he said low enough for just the four of them to hear. "Son, at your back, is a whole lot of firepower. And I know for a fact," he said as he lifted his hand and four red laser dots hit his palm, "contrary to how pretty these lights are, they get ugly real fast. They also show you just how truthful I'm being. You need to put that gun away. Because those little dots"—the laser points moved away from him—"are now parked on you and your brother's backs." He sighed and met the gunman's eyes. "Don't make that happen. Not only would it be a damn shame, and you'd die, but the blood will get all over my new boots. And I'd hate that."

Evan would have to admit, if the cowboy had one thing going

for him, he knew what to say and when to say it. He was able to adapt to any situation and adjust as needed. The man didn't always choose to do it, though. He was a professional level shit-stirrer.

"Jess, it's fine."

Turning slowly, Evan faced the brothers, putting the gun muzzle at his own stomach. "I told you I would help. I've cut a deal for you both. You won't escape jail time, but I have a very good lawyer waiting to defend you both and fully paid to do an aggressive as legally possible to defend you. He owes me a favor. I'll also testify in your defense if he advises me to, about how you took measures not to harm the hostages. And how surrendering was your choice. Be honest and tell them the robbery went wrong. You never meant for it to go as it did. I believe the court will give some leniency." He held his hand out toward Charlie. "The offer will be null and void if you shoot me. Hand me the gun. Do as we ask, and I promise you," he said as his gaze slid to Kyle, "I make a vow to do all I can to help you."

Jess angled his head to add to Evan's list of offerings. "And I know about your girl. Her being pregnant. I'll make sure she's taken care of. Evan and I have been where you boys are now. Let us help you. It ain't goin' to do anyone any good if this all goes tits up to tragic."

"Charlie, they will take care of Mary," Kyle pleaded and put his hand on top of the gun. "Listen to them, big brother."

Charlie swung his focus to Kyle, and the two men exchanged some silent agreement. When the gun slapped into Evan's palm, both Evan and Jess blew out a breath of stress as they let it go.

"This better be on the up-and-up." Charlie swallowed as he spoke. Resignation and exhaustion seemed to snuff out his cocky bravado. "And if it is, then thank you. Both of you." He put his hands on the top of his head, then Kyle followed, and both men went to their knees.

Jess gave Evan a look expressing a level of relief likely a tenth of his own. The cowboy moved to place the cuffs on the brothers and hauled both to their feet. Police officers swarmed to take the men into custody. Detective Bailey supervised that the brothers were handled with respect. Neither man gave the police a reason not to.

Watching them go, Evan let his exhaustion call the shots and he lowered his head. The sun touched the tips of his boots. Habit led him to take a step back and sink to sit on the store's doorway even though the shadows gave him safety.

"You know, E." The cowboy moved to sit next to him. "That was about the bravest thing I ever did see. You were one slight push from going crispy. I was even preparin' myself to pinch my nose to avoid smelling the stench."

Evan fell back to lay on the floor. The cool tile soothed his aching muscles. He hurt from head to toe, and his skin stung from being so close to the sunlight. "I almost thought we'd both learn how painful it would be. I'm glad we'll continue to wonder."

Jess chuckled with a smile, and then it fell. "Lily left. She was real upset, E. I don't think it was personal."

Evan barked out a weak laugh and brought his arms up to fold over his forehead. "That's where you're wrong, Bailey. With her, it's as personal as it gets."

## 2 O

ONE WEEK LATER

*L*ily called in sick with the flu after the robbery. She came down with the illness in the past, but it was the only excuse she could think of. She needed to nurse her broken heart, needed some time to lick her pride. She was embarrassed enough. No need to make a public show of her dragging it around like a ball and chain of shame. By now, she knew all of the Grid knew about her and Evan. The rumor mill at work ground out news faster than a waiter sprinkling parmesan cheese on her salad at Olive Garden.

However, Lily found a reason to be proud of herself, too. Rather than dive into food for comfort as she had done in the past, she took up the ritual of running. Day. Morning. Evening. Nights. It kept her away from the Ben & Jerry's that called out to her from the freezer. She cleared off the laundry and books from her treadmill and finally used it daily. She drove herself to the point of exhaustion. She and her dog slept hard at night. If only the exercise held sway on the dreams.

The nightmares from her parents' and brother's deaths she

had grown accustomed to. When she woke from those, she'd pick up whatever book she was reading at the time from the nightstand and get lost in someone else's world to escape her own until sleep became more welcoming. Since the robbery, a new type of dream woke her. They made her angry but frustratingly turned on, too.

Visions of Evan above her as his face twisted in climax. His abs as she clawed at him. The taste of him in her mouth. The way his kisses caused her brain to black out. To devote all body processes to feel more of him as he pushed and pulled inside of her.

Okay, maybe those should be classified as nightmares. She hated them more. She woke up a mess. She ranted. Then she cried. Ranted more and then fell asleep, sobbing like a girl stood up at prom. *That* made zero sense. Lily never went to prom. She'd never been asked to any school dances.

Her sisters called to check on her throughout the week. Did she feel better? She told them she did, but no, she still felt terrible. Was she taking meds? Sure! Hah, as if one existed for the O'Brien flu. Liquids? Rest? A couple of shots of Maker's Mark counted as fluids, right? Rest, sure. Around the wet spots in dreams with Evan.

Jess and Beth called. Desi too. During each conversation, she avoided discussing the robbery or Evan. She used a dismissive, no big deal attitude to detour the conversation and keep them from asking. Almost as humiliating as being used and rejected by Evan was talking about being used and rejected by the asshole.

---

"Evan, you with us?"

Evan led the weekly squad leader status meeting every Wednesday. Normally, a quick hour of clipped top-level intel of current issues. He'd end it with a small reminder for the fighters to watch their six and their assigned Relays to get everyone home in the morning alive.

All week, his head had been a wreck. Most everyone assumed a short-term case of PTS from the robbery. Figuratively they would be correct but also indirectly wrong. He suffered no ill effect from the robbery itself. The Grid psychiatrist, Skyler Wyatt noted such in Evan's file and cleared him for regular duty. Evan somehow pulled off being focused and clearheaded during the session. Every other activity was a tangled mess of emotions. He lectured himself a dozen times an hour. He performed the chore again when his mind drifted off during the meeting. And everyone, the men and women under his command, had noticed. He could see it in their amused expressions. "No. Dismissed."

"So…"

Oh good god, the last thing Evan needed was Lily's brother-in-law Reno nosing around in the relationship, or lack of, between him and Lily. "Do you not know what the word *dismissed* entails, Keeper?"

Giving Reno a vicious side-eye as the man took roost on the corner of Evan's desk, he knew the man wouldn't go away. Evan faced him. Might as well get this over. A fresh bottle of Maker's Mark for dinner waited for Evan at home. "If you are here to discuss Lily and me, don't. There is zero to discuss. We aren't a couple. We won't be a couple. Nothing to talk about."

"Gee. How did you know?" Reno wiggled a brow upward with a smirk. "I heard alllll of that." He circled a finger around Evan's face. "But why not?"

Maybe Evan was wrong. Maybe Reno would go away if ignored. He went back to standing bent over his desk to write notes in his planner. To scroll through the tablet where status updates posted on the internal system. Yet Reno stayed. He contemplated the possibility of making origami out of Post-it notes, but it would be a waste of both time and the budget. Reno would not get the clue that he should give up and go. The man needed instructions drawn in crayon on most days.

Sighing, Evan pivoted to sit on the edge of his desk next to the man. After he crossed his arms and ankles, he looked over at

Reno. "There is a multitude of reasons why not. I have zero time. My job is my sole focus. *Sole* means *only*, in case that special brain of yours needs a definition as it does with the word *dismissed.*"

Reno responded with a mischievous grin. "Also, the bottom of a shoe. And that soul is what makes us all alive and stuff. Well, not spelled the same, but they sound the same. Sole, soul." His blue eyes oscillated around the room and back. "You know what I mean." He pointed to Evan as he pulled a package of Twizzlers from his jacket pocket, slapped it on his tongue, and spun the candy with his fangs. "I'm just wondering. You're Grid. She's Grid. You're single. She's single. You two banged. From what I hear, you bit her." He pulled the licorice free to wiggle it in Evan's direction. "Did she bite you back? I know her sister *loves* to bite. Claw too. And those sounds—"

Evan could see the man's brain take a happy trip to someplace Evan dared not follow regarding the man's wife. He had already gone there with her sister—no need to have a postcard to remember.

"Stop." Evan brought a hand up to knead his forehead. "Can we save the *always fun with words* game for another time?" He rubbed the back of his neck. "Lily is amazing. Incredible. Beautiful. Strong. Brave. She irritates the hell out of me. Confrontational and argumentative. Other men would find that annoying. I find it challenging. The issue is not her. It's me."

"Ah, the whole *it's not you, it's me* excuse. Evan..." Reno pushed off the desk to stand in front of him. "Listen to all those things you *just* said. You described the perfect woman for you. Or did you not realize it? I will ask this again. Why not?"

Evan opened his mouth to respond, but how could he? Reno's words struck on the truth. Lily had every quality in a woman Evan should be with. That Evan would want. And fuck, did he want her, had for years. Swallowing, his chin hit his chest as he looked to the floor. "It's impossible. I can't risk her." He angled his head sideways to Reno. "And I won't risk losing her to this war. To the violence and the trauma that is this world we're in."

*What being with him and the huge target on his back would bring to her.*

Reno nodded, pressed his lips together, and Evan took the man's silence as agreement. Yippy. An easy end to their discussion. Until Reno continued. Dammit. Wrong again.

"But Evan, she's already in it. So are you. There's a reason we don't date outside of the Grid. It's close to impossible. What's the point? We can't be ourselves. Heck, there's no fun with fangs on those that don't know about them. It freaks people out. They usually scream. Loud." He snorted. "Okay, sure Jess pulled off hooking up with a civilian. Beth is amazing. But she's also the exception to history and typical relationship rules."

Reno's voice softened. His hand came up to rest on Evan's shoulder. "But E, love also strengthens us and makes us willing to continue the fight. When this war is over, wouldn't it be nice to have someone who made the victory worth it?" Reno's hand squeezed before he moved it and placed a fingertip on Evan's forehead. "But, hey, you can be the stupid one for once." He smiled. "I'll loan you the T-shirt that I get to wear *all* the time since I hold the title."

"We all can't be you, Reno. We can only wish to find the love you have."

Reno scrunched up his face as he stepped back. "Or maybe, you need to stop wishing and take the love you already have for someone"—he coughed—"Lily. And let her decide if she wants it. You can't make all the choices, E. It's very rude."

Reno smiled, spun and headed for the door. "Just remember, Evan…" He hit the door with his rear to open it. "Love has a way. Just don't get slaughtered to make it happen. I don't recommend it. It leaves a mark, it's messy, and you go through so many Boo-Boo Kitty bandages."

"O'Brien."

Evan had finished testifying for Kyle and Charlie. Not for the prosecution, however, but for the defense as a character witness. Evan kept his word, even if it meant arranging an evening hearing so he could. When the rich baritone voice called his name, he pivoted to see Reznor Maine.

They reached each other in the courtroom hallway to shake hands. "I thought you returned to Sunnyville?"

Rez nodded. "I did. And I should have guessed having court at night involved you and your NDA-covered details I won't bring up or talk about. I'd like to continue breathing. It's a habit I enjoy." The man smiled. "I came back to do my part as a witness. But I cut those two idiots some slack." He brought a hand up to hold his finger and thumb slightly apart. "A micro amount. But it's more than I'd usually do. Desi told me how they didn't hurt anyone. And once I got over being pissed about the situation, I heard her out." He snorted. "My girl is hard to say no to, but she was also right."

"You have an outstanding woman. I read the reports." Evan glanced around. "Did she come with you to San Fran?"

"She did. She's meeting a friend. I thought perhaps you and I could grab some coffee. Have some chitchat over dinner and pass the time." Rez put his arm around Evan's shoulders to turn him toward the exit. "I'd make that an order, but something tells me you are higher up in the food chain in your world than I am in mine since going to Sunnyville." He gave Evan a shit-eating grin. "For now."

Evan chuckled as he was led to the parking lot. "A friend, huh…"

<hr>

"This is nice, Desi. And this wine and cheesecake? A-mazing." Desi called Lily a few days ago. She and Reznor needed to come back to the city to tie up the court details of the robbery. They met up at the Cheesecake Factory and hugged for the longest time in the foyer. Lily welcomed the time to meet her friend and a chance to have the first dessert in two weeks. If one broke a diet, they should do it with some of the best cheesecake in the city.

"It is. I love coming here whenever we come to San Fran. The company really needs to open a branch back home." Desi stabbed a forkful of dessert, put it in her mouth, and let out a moan of pleasure. "It's not as good as sex with Rez, but it's close." She gave Lily a wink. "How's Evan?"

Lily's fork of cheesecake paused halfway to her mouth. She lifted her brows before completing the move. "I wouldn't know."

Desi set her fork down and sipped her wine. She looked at Lily over the rim of the glass. "Really? You two work together. Live in the same city. And you have no idea how he is?"

Lily shoved more cheesecake in her mouth. So much for restarting her diet. Again. She'd place the blame on Evan. All his fault she just nosedived into her comfort food habit after resolving to leave toxic ones behind. "Desi." She swallowed and regarded her friend. "It would never work out with Evan. We're night and day. And I have enough pride, even if it's small and wavers most days, to not go after him. We suffered a weak mutual moment in an awful situation." She took a long drink of her wine. "With Evan"—her fingers came up to brush over the healing bite on her neck—"it's *literally* a case of once bitten, twice shy."

Desi reached over to press her hand over Lily's on the table. "Look, I get it. From what you told me and I saw for myself, Evan might be a long-lost Malone brother. They are just a stubborn bunch. I remember when Emmy, my bestie, and Grant Malone crossed paths. Both of them fought their attraction. And their relationship, in the beginning, wasn't an easy one. I will admit, I attempted some unwanted matchmaking moves. Which I also denied."

She laughed. "But now they are so happy. I will also confess I had to hide my envy. I was thrilled for them. No one deserved it more. I began to believe I would be one of those women who would always be a bridesmaid and never a bride. Not that I wanted marriage. Or commitment. But I wanted that deep of a relationship. Feeling like that got old. I became resigned. Until one day, Reznor Maine rented the house next to mine. Lordy, that man was so hot. We're talking H.A.W.T. hot. All that brawn mixed with intensity. It's strange how men who do dangerous jobs become dangerously appealing. Like an invisible layer of wildness forms on them from dealing with life and death situations and surviving. It adds a special kind of sex appeal." She chuckled and sat back to swirl the wine in its glass. "And he knew it. He worked it doing the simplest tasks like putting away my trash cans, mowing my grass. Sure, he blew it off that he was just neighborly. But there is no way he didn't know how he looked. Strutting, doing what he considered a man's duty. Sexy and all male."

---

LILY APPRECIATED Desi's encouragement and retell of her personal history. But she wasn't her friend. Not even close. And Evan was night and day compared to Reznor, from what she could tell. She rolled her eyes. "I can put away my own trash cans. And the older man that does my yard work needs the money. His wife has cats to support." She was looking to the side and regretted taking that direction.

A cheerful couple sat in a booth by the windows. The man spoke in hushed tones, and the woman erupted in joy by what he said. She threw her arms around him, and he slipped a ring on her finger. He stood up and stated proudly to the rest of the diners. "We're getting married!" The crowd broke out in cheers of congratulations and applause.

"Do you want to get married again?"

Lily swung her focus back to Desi. "Of course I do. Just like you were envious of your best friend, I'm envious of my sisters. Both married. Kids. I tried it. I failed at it. Another lesson I care not to repeat."

Desi tilted her head. "I'm the same way. Well, without the first divorce aspect. I told Reznor that. He agreed. For now, it's not for us. But Lily..." She scooted around the semi-circle booth to sit next to her. "You don't want marriage. Okay. But are you going to tell me you don't want love? Or at *least* try in case it's right in front of you?"

Lily stared at Desi and cleared her throat. The truth of her friend's words hit her broadside. T-boned her off her orbit of resolve, actually, and it wasn't very stable before. "But he doesn't want love with me. And right in front of me? No. You don't know Evan. He'll never be the one to step up and do what Reznor did for you. He's not the type to declare love first." She poured herself more wine. "He's not the type to declare it all."

Desi leaned against her. "Then he's a fool. Or you are. Or you both are." She laughed, and Lily tried to. But it was tough to pull off when all she wanted was to cry for the rest of her lonely days.

<hr>

"TELL me about this Lily woman. Desi's friend."

"You mean the one your girlfriend is having dinner with?" Evan smirked. "I hope you don't play poker, Maine." Evan had recommended they eat at Ms. Woo's Noodle shop. Not only did the older woman make the best Vietnamese Pho, but she was also retired from Grid and provided a private room for anyone working for it. After she served heaping, steaming bowls of noodle soup, wontons, and coffee, she left him and Reznor to talk.

Evan wrapped noodles around a pair of chopsticks and shrugged. "What is there to tell? She's bossy, annoying, loud, and stubborn. She grates on my nerves, pushes my patience, and likes to challenge me. On everything. Every. Damn. Thing." He ate the bite and spoke as he chewed. "She's generational in that place you're not allowed to talk about and—" He swallowed and used another shrug rather than say more. "Anyway, not much to tell."

"Hmm. Is she beautiful? Sexy? A woman a guy wouldn't get bored with? And one he'd want to keep in his bed forever?" Reznor snorted. "I'm starting to understand why she and my girl are such good friends. Besides loving fur-kids more than us mere men some days."

"First, you're putting words in my mouth about her. I said none of that." Evan snorted in amusement and chuckled. "And I think you using the word *fur-kid* just dropped your alpha-male credit down a few points."

Reznor laughed. "I gave in. It was that, or she let every damn dog and cat she has in her house into the bed. It wouldn't leave any room for my big ass. And in Desi's bed is where I always want it to be." He ate some noodles. "You were right. These are good."

"May I ask you a question?" Evan slid his empty bowl away as he sat back. "You have a job similar to mine. I bet you have the same mindset. It's dangerous. We could die at any moment on any given day. And as much as we tell ourselves that we won't take that shit home with us, it follows, creeps around the edges, hides in the shadows of the backyard. It's impossible not to."

"Bullshit."

Evan's brows shot up. "It's not. You of all people can't say that. Our worlds are not that different."

Reznor stabbed a wonton and spun it slowly. "Let me elaborate on that, O'Brien. You apparently are solid in that belief. I used to be the same. Sex, a good time. Escape. Drinking. Then going in, strapping on heat, and doing the job, getting it done. Rinse. Repeat. Same thing. Routine has a certain safety in it." He popped the wonton into his mouth. "Until I heard a woman screaming pussy across a backyard."

Evan had been mid-chew. He choked on noodles with Reznor's last statement. "Excuse me? What?"

Reznor laughed. "I shit you not. The very first time I saw my Desi, she was chasing a wet cat. A cop's cat. By the name of Pussy." He picked up another wonton. "Her hair was damp and wild. Face flustered. Attitude and posture yelled bossiness. It was sexy as hell, and it intrigued me. And perhaps I became a little obsessed. I had never met a woman like her. I knew her best friend, who was pregnant with my buddy Grant's baby. Married and happy. He was like us until he met Emmy. I thought it wasn't for me. Just like you." He sipped his coffee. "And she wanted nothing to do with me. Kept me at arm's length. And I tried every damn trick in my thick book of dealing with women to get past her defenses." He chuckled. "I went to Sunnyville for a much needed mental health vacay. The stress of the job was eating me alive. Signed up to teach a self-defense class. Imagine my surprise to see the cat wrangler, my sexy neighbor in the class." He smirked. "It took balls of steel not to grope her as I taught her how to get out of holds, which I wished I had possessed when we got to that part of the course. But anyway..." He pointed his chopsticks at Evan. "She came to my door, we had incredible sex, and that should have been the end."

Evan frowned. The replay of Lily leaving at the store surfaced in his mind. "She walked away, Reznor. She didn't give us a chance. Even if I had wanted one, she decided it was the end. Not me."

Reznor nodded. "As I said, our women are alike. Desi made it clear she didn't want a relationship. She had her insecurities. Hated showing any vulnerabilities. I had my own. Betting you do too. I gave her what she wanted and left. Part of me was tired of trying. She kept pushing me away. Point taken." He poured them both another cup of coffee. "But I could not get that woman out of my head. I tried to use the tried-and-true method of throwing myself back into the job." He smirked with a knowing expression. "But methods only last until replaced by something else better. And it wasn't a problem of Desi being in my head."

He nailed Evan with a serious look. "She was in my heart. And distractions, doubts, coping bullshit tactics can't reach there. None of it worked. I think when someone reaches a heart, one that hardened itself so long to prevent anyone from getting inside, it doesn't let them out. They're there for good. Meant to last or not." Reznor stood, pulled out his wallet, and dropped cash on the table.

"We never have to pay here," Evan picked up the bills and handed them back to Reznor.

"Damn, you got some real perks in your world that I'm not supposed to know about." He chuckled. "Although Desi *did* ask if there was a way to get some fangs. She finds them sexy."

Evan stood to exit with the man, and Rez clapped a hand on his shoulder. "Look. I know where you're at in this. How deciding to be with someone is perhaps one of the hardest decisions you'll have to make. And that's knowing we both deal with life-ending situations in our jobs. But the thing with love is this. Love doesn't give a crap about our priorities or duty. It just wants to find a home in our heart with someone it knows is meant to be there."

Evan narrowed his eyes. "You've been talking to someone I work with? Shorter than us. Leaner. Brilliant blue eyes and has the maturity of a twelve-year-old?"

Reznor laughed as they reached the door. "I don't believe I have, why?"

Evan reached his car and shrugged. "I don't know. He said pretty much the same thing. Funny, I never knew he could actually be *wise*."

*L*ily's favorite movie was *He's Not That Into You*. Since the episode, activity, sexual aerobics, or whichever words applied to what happened with her and Evan, she identified with the flick more than ever.

Lily expected Emma any minute to bring the kids over. She looked forward to spending time with her niece and nephew. Reno and Emma rarely had nights out with their jobs. She was happy to babysit so they could and had snack and craft supplies set up on the table ready. Lily loved the kiddos. She still wore the clothes she worked out in earlier since the crafts she and the kids made were fun but messy.

Hearing the doorbell, she hopped up with her shepherd at her heels and jogged to the door. "Coming! You guys are a little early. I thought the movie didn't start until—" She swung the door open, and the dog started barking. Her sister and family were *not* the ones standing on Lily's stoop.

Evan was.

"Nope." She tried to close the door in his face. She shook her head, swayed her hips, and walked back inside. "Not tonight. Not tomorrow. And not the day after that." Turning, she found he had invaded her space anyway. He squatted down to pet the dog. One who would have made its master happy if it bit Evan's hand. She smirked and mumbled, "Traitor."

"Seems like a loyal enough dog." He chuckled. "Ah, you weren't talking about the dog. Noted. And deserved."

He stood, and she rested a hip on the back of her couch. She couldn't care less about wearing her comfy clothes. Screw him. She wasn't wearing a lick of makeup either. He could bite himself if he didn't like her hair in a messy bun because he sure as hell would not be biting her. Not again. Even if the thought of it made her want to scissor her legs to stop the ache at the junction of them. He wasn't the only man in her circle with fangs. And a handsome face. Hazel eyes. Abs she wanted to lick.

*God, Lily, stop. Get him out of your head. Out of your house. Quick.*

"Why are you here? I don't believe I invited you to my home. In fact, I'm sure you're smart enough to know I've been avoiding you because I *don't* want to see you, Mr. O'Brien." Lowering her head, she crossed her arms over her chest. "We have no reason to see each other outside of work. I'll email my reports. Isn't it what you asked me to do repeatedly? Request fulfilled."

"Lily. I asked Reno to run interference."

Her head snapped up to glare at him. Oh, she would kick her brother-in-law in the balls so hard that he'd never have another baby with her sister.

"Before you get pissed, they are still coming. He disclosed they were having a date night and asked for the evening off. I know you normally watch the children, so I asked him if I could see you before they arrived."

Lily squeezed her eyes shut. She felt the sting of tears behind her eyelids. She would be damned if she cried in front of him, showing him the effect he still had on her—might always have on her, the residue of being with him forever left behind on her heart.

"Evan, please. I can't do this with you. I don't want to talk about it. I don't want to relive it." She opened her eyes and brought a hand up to wipe the tears angrily. "And I'm pretty sure you don't want that, either." She swallowed and came close to sobbing. "Just go."

Evan took a step toward her. She took one back. "Lily, listen to me. When you walked away—"

"Oh no, you don't! You were being stupid. You were about to step into the sun! You put yourself in front of those two morons that held me, Beth, and my friend *hostage*!" She wasted zero effort to wipe the second wave of tears. "What was I supposed to do? Watch you die? I mean, I've had guys ghost me. Send me excuses after screwing once, but *none* got themselves shot and killed to avoid dealing with me!" She stomped up to him and shoved him. "Get. Out."

"I'm trying to explain it to you. If you would just—"

"Just what, Evan? Listen? Why? What good would it do me? Oh, wait." She jerked and let out a tearful laugh. "Did you come by here to break up with me? Is that how they did it forever-fucking-ever ago?" She snorted and shook her head. "Unbelievable! Well, sweet cheeks, there's no need for that in modern times. I am a big girl. A grown-ass woman. I know what happened between us meant nothing."

"No, there is no reason to break up. I wanted to tell you—"

She cut him off again. He approached a second time. This time, she scooted back so fast she almost fell over the sofa. Regaining her stability, she pointed her finger at him. "Oh, what, E? To be safe? Like you tell me every time rather than say goodbye? You never say goodbye. It's always that bullshit." She mocked his Irish accent and tone. "Be safe. Yada, yada, blah, blah."

"For fuck's sake, Lily. Would you just—"

His voice betrayed his irritation. She irritated him. Annoyed him. Didn't he call that a challenge? Oh sure, he called it that when he wanted to get her clothes off.

"Oh, *you* don't get to say the f-word to me! In fact, that will never come *up* between us again." She stepped up to him with a smirk and swayed her head. "And I lied about you being in the top five in the dick pick pool. You weren't even close."

Evan narrowed his eyes before moving to her. No escaping him the third time. The sofa behind her would have sent her flipping feet over head. He came toward her, leaving a narrow inch or two between them. Lily's focus went from his eyes to his bared fangs and up again. Her throat went dry. Her nose took in the clean male scent of him. And all that muscle. Her hands ached to rake her nails over each one again.

"I wish you would listen to me. Just shut up and listen. If you still want me to go, I'll go. If you never want to see me again. Fine. You won't. But you, Ms. Devenmore, will stand there and listen if you want to get those wishes."

"It's Lily," she snarled through her clenched teeth. "And fine. Talk. And make it quick. The movie is almost over."

EVAN GAVE up trying to insert his own reasoning into her tirade. Maybe if she vented, she would run out of steam and not only let him speak but listen. When she did, he snorted, then reached over, picked up the remote, and hit pause. "There. No longer an issue."

The last thing Evan wanted to do was fight with her. Nor be the cause of her tears. She didn't need to know he had paced his house all day waiting for the sun to set. To come here and do what he had decided to do, what he *needed* to do. He should have known the woman would have her defenses up as high as they could go. He couldn't blame her. His had been up for two weeks. Walls she climbed before he struggled and failed to build again. Brick by brick, they crumbled at just the thought of Lily Devenmore.

Reno's rare wisdom had staying power. Why not Lily Devenmore? No other woman on the planet equaled her. She was beautiful and wild. Brave and strong. A challenge, never dull, and she caused a stirring in his cock whenever she looked at him. Even as she did now. Furious and indignant. Stubborn. And after seeing her in a fresh light through the darkness of his past, his heart was hers before Evan could even try to stop her ownership.

Reznor's advice stuck, as well—once Lily had found a way inside his heart, there was no getting her out. Evan would do whatever it took so that she never wanted to. A bold, loud, beautiful bird of fantasy, willingly staying inside of a dented cage without a door, choosing to be there for him to cherish forever because she did.

He brought his hands up to cup her face and met her eyes. "Now, I want you to be quiet. Please." Licking his lips, he swallowed. This was harder than he had predicted when he rehearsed this scene for hours—boosting his bravery to say it and have her understand. If she still wanted to. She tensed under his touch. She expected an emotional blow from him.

He, in turn, braced for her rejection. He would suffer a hit of his own making by rejecting her first. They were so much alike. Why he hadn't he seen it before... maybe he was blind, after all.

"The reason I say stay safe is it's my duty caring about everyone. I abhor goodbyes. We lose so many in this war. It's become a normal thing. I'm callous to it after a century. But for years, the thought of my life without you in it hurt. Never facing off with you in another disagreement is dreadful. To not have you mouthing back to piss me off, unimaginable. Lily, you were right. I was a coward to not let anyone into my life." He lowered his head, and they shared a breath as he brought his lips right above hers to whisper, "But it's all changed to so much more. And I believe you know it too."

Lily blinked. She sputtered. And blinked many times more.

He couldn't help but smile. "Why, Ms. Devenmore, have I made you speechless?"

"Evan, if you're saying this just to get in my pants again..." Her eyes went down, and she blushed in the most delightful way. He felt the heat of it under his palms. "If I were *wearing* pants and not these shorts that make my legs look awful—and I wish I had shaved."

He chuckled. "Baby, do you really think I need to say sweet words to get your"—he angled his head to follow her previous visual path in amusement—"legs in those shorts, stubby hair or not, around my waist again, we know you lie. I didn't need to before." He ran his knuckles along her jaw, and his thumb grazed her bottom lip. "I'll prove that when I'm done if you'd like."

"You give your powers of seduction too much credit, O'Brien," she said with a snort.

He caught her wrist as her hand came over to slap him. His hips angled to avoid her knee as it went for his balls. "You should know that when you pretend to fight me, it only turns me on. Stop distracting me, woman."

She smirked, and he cleared his throat. "Lily. I think you're beautiful. Intelligent. And I want you in my life. Not as a subordinate. Or a combatant that drives me insane more often than not. I want you—" He brought her hand to his heart. "I had rehearsed saying I want you here. But Lily, you're already deep inside my heart. With each beat. And it hurt when you walked away—every single step. I considered willing the sun to reverse its path and reach me. For a nervous, trigger finger twitching sniper to let a bullet fly. Seeing you go, I wanted to die rather than live without you to drive me crazy. To let you in. To love you."

Lily sniffed and failed to regain her composure. "That would have been crazy. And I would have been pissed at you. Sought your sorry ass in Hell to make you pay for being a moron." Apparently, her sarcasm had no problem staying intact.

"I know. I would have spent the rest of my tortured eternity waiting for the devil to release me because you aggravated the piss out of him with your demands that he do just that." He softly kissed each track of her tears with a smile. "If only to bitch me out and send me back to be tortured more."

She took a deep breath. So deep, Evan felt her shudder. "I *do* want you to stay safe." He pulled back and wanted to fall into her beautiful green eyes. "But I want you to stay safe with *me*. With each other. Together. I want to kiss you before I go to work. I want to get chains of text from you to distract me from my duty. I'd even love if they bitch at me. Have those stupid emojis. As long as I know you'll be in my life, day and night. I want to make love to you. And then go wild and fuck you in my office. I want to make you laugh. Hold you when you cry. I have immortal life. But I don't want to waste another single moment without you driving me crazy and making you love me. As much as I already do you."

She cried harder, and her free hand balled up and punched him in the chest.

"Ouch." He grunted in response.

"Evan! Why did you say all that?"

He sputtered, frowned, and brought a hand up. "Why? Well, I—"

But Lily threw her arms around his neck, and when her mouth meshed with his, he completely forgot the question. Or an answer. Whichever he was responsible for. He lost himself in her kiss. He picked her up in his arms and loved how her legs wrapped around him like a vice. The move went straight to his loins, hardening by the time she crossed her ankles on his ass.

Keeping her there, he pulled back. "Am I to take it you want the same? That you feel for me in the same manner?"

She laughed through her tears and nodded. "Yes. I do. I have. I will—all the things. And you didn't need to say all that. I mean, it was nice, but a waste of time. All I wanted to hear and all you had to say was you loved me. Because I love you—that's why I was afraid that day at the store. I loved you. And the thought of losing you, seeing what I lost before I really had it. Watching you die would be more than I could take." She laid her forehead on his shoulder. "That's me being a coward. I guess we're even."

Chuckling, he kissed her again. "I have a caveat to our being together."

Lily jerked back in his arms. Her head angled, and her gaze narrowed. "Are you seriously going to put conditions on our relationship? You want this over before we even get to the wonderful stuff? For that matter, the first date?" She rolled her eyes. "Old water, expired MREs, and a dusty bunker with gunmen wanting to put more holes in you does not classify as a date, Evan O'Brien."

Evan laughed and shook his head. "Not a condition. More of a request." He put his finger on her nose. "Hear me out, baby."

She kept her face closed off, doubt clouding her eyes. "Okay, since you called me baby. I like that. You should only use that from now on." She smiled. "It's definitely better than," she mimicked his voice, "Ms. Devenmore." She noticed his patient expression. "Fine. But am I going to need to slap you again?"

Evan grinned wickedly. "You can, but only in your bed. I don't even know where it is, but that can wait." Brushing her hair back, he whispered, "I never want to hear you belittle yourself. Put yourself down. Not to me. Not to anyone. And most importantly, not to yourself. If someone can't see your value, the incredible woman that is Lily Devenmore, they have no worth and don't deserve a moment of our time. If you believe you aren't beautiful, let me know. All you have to do is see yourself through my eyes." He smiled. "And as we have established, I am not blind. My love isn't either. It sees all of you—every single part. The insides you try to hide. The outside you use to cover it up. The vulnerable and the scared. The weak and the strong. And my soul isn't deaf. It can hear the pureness of yours, even when your words and bravado try to shelter its song." He rumbled a playful growl and nibbled her neck. "We'll address my other senses later."

Lily was speechless, giddy, and awash with fear all at the same dizzying time. Evan O'Brien loved her and wanted to be with her. Her. In every way. Just as she was. Complicated and all. Brushing her fingers through his hair, she let her head fall back as he teased her throat with those sinful fangs of his.

"Evan, wait. Before you make me go brain dead in bed." His head lifted, and she met his eyes as he lowered her to the floor. "I can't promise my doubts won't rise to cause us problems. I've had them for so long. I gave them reign, and sometimes, no matter how much I want to, they control me. But I want to try.

For you. Just know that some days, I'm a bitch. Other days, I can't stand myself. Are you sure you want all of that?" She hesitated to say more—was she saying too much? Did she just scare him off? She needed to be honest if this was going to work. But would he no longer want it to? "It's fine if you don't. I much rather stop this now than later when I won't survive you leaving me."

He sighed and pressed his lips together. Lily's heart clenched. No man would want a woman with so much baggage. Not a man like him. *Why hadn't she just kept her mouth shut?*

"There will be some days I come home to you bloody. Battered, bruised. Shot." His head went down as he spoke. "I'll be angry. Raw and defensive. Bark and bitch." Lily could see his jaw work as he ground his fangs. "Battle and work at times make me unapproachable. I wish to be left alone. I won't want to talk. I may not want to be seen. I have nightmares. I have paranoia when I feel threatened. I become fierce when I feel backed into a corner." His head came up to meet her eyes. "But I want nothing more than to take you as you are, Lily Devenmore. If you wish to try and do the same for me." He swallowed and grasped her chin in his fingers. "We shall handle each other. And we'll learn to do together."

Lily smiled and nodded before she lifted on her toes and kissed him. "Together. Now, my turn for some rules."

She hopped back up, and Evan caught her with ease. "Rules? So soon? We haven't been in a relationship for five minutes. You complained about my putting a caveat, and now you want rules?" He began walking, and Lily pointed down the hall toward the direction of her bedroom.

Lily giggled and nuzzled his neck. "Yup. I have to be on top during sex at least twice a week."

Evan's steps faltered. "I can agree to that. It's a delightful view. One of my favorites."

"Good." She played with the hair at the nape of his neck. "And I want you to be nude as much as possible." She smiled and shrugged. "Here. Or your place. You can wear clothes to work and in public."

He halted with a throaty laugh. "I will agree to that rule, as well." He raised a brow. "As long as it also applies to you."

Lily blushed shyly before she nodded. And recovered her wickedness in a blink. "As long as you worship me like a goddess, I'll agree."

He chuckled as they reached her bedroom door. "And I'll let you continue to think that a blow job is both a tactic to stall and your superpower."

Lily gasped, her jaw dropping. "You, how… I didn't say that out loud."

Evan smiled. "I know. And yes, I can read minds."

She knew it! Dang it. She had a lot to learn about the man she loved, and he a lot to learn about her. She was an educator, after all. Adding naked education to her personal lesson plan had a certain appeal.

**The End**

**No Sun Needed**

Want to keep up with all of the other books
in K. Bromberg's Everyday Heroes World?

You can visit us anytime at http://www.kbworlds.com/
and the best way to stay up to date on all of our latest releases and
sales, is to sign up for our official KB Worlds newsletter here:
https://smarturl.it/KBWNewsletter.

Are you interested in reading the bestselling books that inspired
the Everyday Heroes World?

You can find them here:
https://www.kbromberg.com/books/everyday-heroes/.

"I am the product of several realities making the whole: a troubled childhood, domestic violence survivor, homeless person, single mother, and a murder/suicide survivor. But in every single one of those realities, one thing remained true—my imagination."

Reading and writing have always been Ms. Ward's escape. And she wants to continue to give that to her readers as well. Known for action, drama, laughter, darkness, and twists you won't see coming in the same book, Ward is known for writing books that are diverse, different, and unique. A bestselling author on both Amazon and ARe Romance, Ms. Ward's books have won awards from various blogs and Preditors and Editors in the categories of reader favorites, best dark romance, and others. Ms.

Ward's books have also been reviewed in Ind'Tale Magazine and been nominated for their prestigious RONE awards.

Born and raised in Texas and spending time living in Kentucky, Ms. Ward spends her days and nights writing as therapy to deal with life and all that it brings—from the past and present. And hopefully finds joy, laughter and fun to mix in with the dark. Something her readers have come to love in her works. She is the proud parent of three very independent grown children and grandmother to three delightful grandchildren. She has four fur babies that sit and ponder why their human is talking to herself late into the night as she writes out colorful and diverse, if not twisted, characters and tales.

LINKS SO WE CAN KEEP IN TOUCH.

Website: www.AuthorJasTWard.com

*You can sign up for my newsletter and get a free read!*

facebook.com/AuthorJasTWard

twitter.com/JasTWard

instagram.com/jast.ward

bookbub.com/authors/jas-t-ward